MY BIRTHDAY GETAWAY

My Holiday Tails

Marina Simcoe

To Janet, Kitty, Ronika, and Avis.

Thank you.

My Birthday Getaway

Chapter 1

Lori

"Bye, asshole!" The young woman, whose name was Felicity Davis according to the passengers list, stomped her foot. "Next time, think twice before abducting an innocent woman who is minding her own business."

She spun on her heel, sending a myriad of long, multi-colored braids flying around her head and shoulders. A male alien watched her with a desolate expression as she headed across the docking deck of the alien ship toward our shuttle from Earth.

Felicity Davis was the first passenger to board my shuttle today. There were supposed to be ten—ten women out of the ninety-seven whom the aliens from the planet Ivodi had abducted during their first two months orbiting the Earth. For the past week and a half, they'd been releasing them all.

"Hey, Lori. There's the commander." Maddy, my First Officer, tipped her chin at the tall Ivodian who'd just come out onto the deck.

My heart skipped a beat, then skidded off at lighting speed.

"Aaaand, you're blushing again," Maddy commented squinting her eyes in a teasing expression.

I couldn't help it. My thirtieth birthday was this Saturday and here I was, crushing on a man like a teenager.

It was impossible not to, though. Commander Nex of the Ivodian ship Conqueror was a sight to behold. Tall and built like a heavy-weight athlete, he commanded attention with his mere presence. I'd been admiring him from the first moment I laid my eyes on him.

He sauntered onto the dock, authority radiating from his figure. The Ivodians' white uniform contrasted with his dark, gray-purple skin. His seven long skinny tails lashed about his legs like whips as he surveyed the dock, arms crossed over his chest.

The commander appeared to be an embodiment of the entire Ivodian race—confident and self-assured to the point of borderline arrogance.

The Ivodians weren't the first alien race who discovered us. The first were Voranians from the planet Neron. Just like the Ivodians, they were interested in our women. But they went about it in a diplomatic way, signing a contract with Earth that allowed women to apply for marriage with a Voranian.

Other nations, such as Ravil from the planet Tragul, had military contracts with Earth.

The Ivodians had shown no interest in diplomacy when they'd first arrived. Their ship, aptly named Conqueror, had appeared in Earth's orbit, guns at the ready. Shocked into stupor by their audacity, the Coalition of the Earth's Governments did nothing for the first several weeks as the Ivodians whizzed around in their sleek flying saucers, snatching women off the streets.

Finally getting their wits about them, the Coalition fought back, demanding the return of all abducted women.

It remained unclear how they'd made the Ivodians comply. Thankfully, despite each party holding the other in the crosshairs, no shots had been fired. The Ivodians had agreed to return all ninety-seven women they'd taken, promising to go back to wherever they had come from in peace.

I'd never had a chance to talk to the commander. I hadn't even met him face-to-face without the windshield of my space shuttle between us. I didn't know his first name, and chances were, I never would. The Ivodian ship was leaving in a couple of weeks, and I'd never see him again.

"You're so cute when you're crushing on a guy," Maddy kept teasing.

"Stupid me," I mumbled, flicking the top button of my teal-blue uniform open. Dress code be damned. I needed some air, and the collar of my shirt suddenly proved too tight.

"We'll need to find a way for the two of you to meet," Maddy added in a more serious tone.

I just shook my head. According to the contract, as the captain of the shuttle, I was supposed to remain on the bridge while docked with the Conqueror. The commander had no reason to ever come on board my shuttle.

In another week or two, all the abducted women would be safely processed and returned to Earth. The Conqueror would leave the orbit, taking its commander away from this planet and out of my life.

He wasn't meant to be anything more than my alien crush.

Maddy picked up the tablet with the paperwork displayed on the screen and clipped on her taser. The company we worked for, Starlight Spacelines, required her to wear the taser when out on the deck. The Ivodians hadn't been hostile to Maddy or me, but the Conqueror was a warship, armed with all kinds of weapons and manned by a crew of fierce warriors. Starlight Spacelines believed a taser would stop them if they chose to attack us.

"Well, I need to go out there now. Do you want me to say hi to the commander from you?" She wiggled her eyebrows.

While the captain remained with the ship at all times, the first officer did what was required outside of the shuttle, including confirming the passenger list, obtaining all signatures, and performing the exterior inspection before take-off. Maddy had met the commander personally and had spoken to him face-to-face.

"Of course not! Don't you dare talk to him about me." I desperately wished my flaming face would cool off or else it risked setting the cockpit on fire. It felt like I was in high school again, crushing on one of the most popular boys in class.

Why did it always have to be the most unattainable one?

Commander Nex had no idea I existed. Most likely, he never would. We only had a handful of scheduled flights left. Once all the abducted women were returned to their homes and families unharmed, the Ivodians would be gone. Besides, did I even want to have anything to do with a man from a race that abducted women, even if they ended up returning them at the end?

The women I've been taking back to Earth appeared to be in good shape. Some even seemed reluctant to leave the Conqueror.

Felicity Davis was obviously not one of those who felt sad about leaving. She marched into the shuttle and tossed her government issued carry-on into the overhead bin.

"Welcome aboard." I smiled, standing at the open door between the bridge and the passenger cabin.

"Hi, Captain." She gave me a friendly grin, plopping into one of the beige leather chairs.

"Happy to be going back home?" I asked. Small talk was not part of my duties, but I was curious.

"Can't wait!" She flicked a handful of braids over her shoulder.

"How long did you spend here?"

"Almost a month!" She shook her head in irritation, shooting a reproachful glare through the window at the Ivodian who'd delivered her to the dock. "Can you believe it? He grabbed me off the street, two blocks away from my house. I had my college final exams that week. I went out for a Slurpee, after studying for hours. And this asshole..." She leaned forward in her seat and yelled toward the open door. "How would you like it if I abducted *you* without asking?"

The gray-purple skin of the Ivodian turned darker over his sharp cheekbones. A row of piercings from the bridge of his nose up to the middle of his forehead glimmered as he shook his head energetically.

"I'd be honored!" he yelled back, loud and clear. "Anyone should be proud to become the spouse of the first engineer of the mighty Conqueror."

Felicity rolled her eyes.

"Hear that? That's what I've been dealing with the entire freaking month. If he's such a catch, why did he need to resort to *stealing* a wife?"

"Are all Ivodians like that?" I asked, forcing my eyes *not* to search for the commander in the crowd gathering on the docking deck.

Felicity shrugged.

"Some are better, some are worse. Just like humans, there're all kinds of Ivodians, I guess. I didn't get to meet many of them. That one," she tipped her head at the first engineer in the window, "kept me locked in his bedroom most of the month. Personally, I don't mind their commander, though. He was the one who finally made it possible for all of us to go home."

My infatuated heart melted at hearing a praise—no matter how slight—for the object of my affection.

"I'm sorry it happened to you," I said with genuine empathy for Felicity's situation.

To my knowledge, the abducted women hadn't been physically or sexually abused. Though, all of them reported enduring forced confinement. Some, like Felicity, had been locked in the bedrooms of their abductors for weeks. I'd even heard rumors of women being chained to their beds.

"Thanks. It's nice to be going home." She blew out a breath, resting against the back of her seat.

Other passengers started to come on board, with Maddy confirming their identities at the door.

"What a mess," Felicity spoke again. "I had a summer job lined up. Now I have to figure out what to do about the exams I never took. I'd just started seeing this guy from my college a month and a half ago.

Such a sweet man. Apparently, he called all over the place, searching for me. My poor parents thought I'd been kidnapped and murdered before the authorities located me..." Her eyes turned glossy with tears, and her smooth, dark skin glowed warmly with the troubling memories.

Not all the boarding women spoke English. Many of those who did nodded in agreement with Felicity. Each had her own abduction story to tell. Though, I also caught a few wistful glances thrown through the windows back at the group of Ivodians who had brought the women to the dock. I wondered if any of the ten women we'd be taking to Earth today would've preferred to stay.

Making sure all had boarded, I went back to my seat in the front.

"All on board." Maddy jumped in the right seat of the First Officer and pulled out the required checklist.

After take-off, I maneuvered the shuttle away from the massive form of the Conqueror and laid the course back to Earth. The latest commercial model of the space shuttle I flew would cover the distance back to my home base near Toronto, Canada in just under two hours.

"Come on, ask," Maddy prodded, the moment we got on course. I let the instruments take over, and we both relaxed a little.

"What?" I feigned innocence, though the question burned on my tongue, begging to be let out.

"You know what I mean," she insisted. "Ask."

"Fine." I gave up pretending and tried not to sound too eager. "Did you get to talk to him?"

"Yes." She beamed.

"And?" I bit my lip in an attempt to hide my anticipation.

"I said 'hi,' and the commander replied 'greetings,'" she blurted out.

"And then?"

Did I need to pull it out from her word by word? Maddy was a chatty type. Surely, she did this on purpose now, to torment me.

"And that's it." She shrugged.

"That's it?"

"Yep. Then, he let the deck supervisor deal with me."

I released the breath I was holding and fought disappointment. Why did it matter what the commander said or didn't say to Maddy? Even if he recited an entire Shakespearian play to her by heart, it wouldn't change my standing with him in any way, whatsoever.

Maddy watched me closely.

"You really have to talk to him, Lori," she said softly. "Friday is our last flight this week. Why don't you ask him to join you in your cottage for your birthday?"

My tiny hunting cabin in the woods could hardly be called a cottage.

"Right, as if he would come," I scoffed.

"You won't know until you ask."

That was the real problem. I wasn't good at talking to strangers, especially those I had a crush on. Even if I got the guts to speak to the commander, I'd most likely just make a fool of myself.

"I'd feel so much better knowing you're not alone out there," Maddy sighed. "In the middle of nowhere."

The cabin my grandpa had built was located on his large property, surrounded by protected land, with not a person in sight for miles. And I loved it that way.

I inherited the cabin after Grandpa passed away, almost exactly a year ago, on my birthday. This Saturday would be especially bittersweet for me this year.

I knew Maddy had wanted to throw me a birthday party in the city. She'd said turning thirty was a huge deal. But all I wanted was to run away and hide in the cabin for a day or two. I'd come back on Monday and deal with everything then, including starting the fourth decade of my life. A party would be too much right now. I needed some space and time for myself.

Surprisingly, sharing the cabin with the commander this weekend didn't sound awful, though. Not at all.

Chapter 2

Lori

"**C**ome on, Lori, what do you have to lose?" Maddy bugged me on our way back to the Conqueror the following Friday.

"Well, my job, for one," I pointed out.

"We won't be breaking any rules."

Maddy had come up with a plan for me to talk to Commander Nex. I could take her place as the first officer to get out of the shuttle. Once I got the passenger list signed off by the deck supervisor, she would check the women's IDs on the shuttle while I'd take the commander aside and...well...talk to him, for once.

"There's no law against the captain leaving the craft while it's docked," Maddy insisted.

"The Ivodians requested I stay with the ship," I argued. "It's in the contract."

"Yeah, but they won't know. I'll give you my hat and my employee pass. We'll trade the epaulettes too. I only can tell the Ivodians apart by the insignia on their sleeves. I'm sure all Earthlings look alike to them, too."

Maddy was half Korean, and I was part Italian, part Scottish, and part who-knew-what-else. Her eyes were dark brown, almost black. Mine were gray or blue, depending on what I was wearing. Her hair was perfectly straight and silky. Mine had a bit of a wave to it. No one from Earth would say we looked the same.

However, she might be right. From the point of view of the aliens, we were two human women of a similar height, dressed in identical teal uniforms, and having long dark hair pulled back in a ponytail—practically indistinguishable. The Ivodians couldn't care less about the differences in our facial features, just like I couldn't really tell the differences in theirs. Except for the commander's features, of course.

When it came to the commander, it was more than just his face. It was the way he conducted himself, in his confident swagger, and his deep, commanding voice that made me weak in my knees whenever I heard him giving orders to his crew.

I would recognize him in a crowd of millions of Ivodians, with or without their insignia.

"When else will you get a chance to speak to him?" Maddy wouldn't quit, tempting me like the serpent of Eden. "Next week is the last flight of our contract. You'll never see him again. It's like now or never, Lori."

"What for, though?" I protested. "He'll leave anyway."

"But the memories will remain!" Maddy exclaimed dramatically. "And the bragging rights. Just think about it, you could be one of the very few women on Earth who's had sex with an Ivodian."

Some of the abducted women had gone that far with their captors, I'd heard.

But me?

I coughed, choking on my breath.

"What *sex*, Maddy? I haven't even agreed to talk to him."

"But you will, won't you?" She batted her eyelashes at me.

"I don't know..." I exhaled.

"Of course you will. What's the worst that can happen? He'd say no, and you'd move on. Oooor..." She stretched the word, deliberately slow. "You'd have steamy-hot alien sex in your cabin all weekend." She wiggled her eyebrows, then added sternly, "Lori, I don't want to spend another week watching you pining after the commander."

"I'm not pining after him," I bristled.

"Oh yeah?" She gave me a look, clearly not impressed by my denial of the obvious.

"I'm just...admiring him, from afar," I explained, fighting the urge to fidget with the name badge clipped to my breast pocket.

"Well, how about *admiring* him while he's lying next to you, in bed, naked? Wouldn't that be better? Give him a chance to give you more to *admire*."

"Maddy!" I glared at her, muttering under my breath, "You know for a first officer, you sure are way too bossy."

She just laughed. "I won't be a First Officer forever. I bet you'll miss me when I'm upgraded to captain next year. I'll be flying with someone else, then."

I didn't argue with that because I knew she was right. I was going to miss her. Maddy was not just a competent pilot and a great friend, she was fun to work with. Of course, most of the time she wasn't this damn pushy. Though, I had to admit, all she was doing was voicing my deepest desires out loud.

"What's in it for you?" I asked. "Why do you want me to talk to him so badly?"

"Aside from having my captain stop blushing and sighing like a schoolgirl?" She leaned closer with a sly smile. "I want to hear a first-hand account of what sex with an Ivodian is like."

I dropped my gaze, afraid to even think about ever going that far with the commander. Just talking to him felt intimidating enough. I'd probably burst into flames if I ever had to get naked in front of him.

"What makes you think I'd tell you?" I mumbled.

"What makes you think I'd have anything to tell?" would have been a more appropriate question.

"Oh, you will." Maddy waved me off. She obviously had more confidence in me than I did. "You always tell me everything. Ooh, do you think he'd spank you with his tails?" She cocked an eyebrow and flashed a naughty smile. "Guess what I heard from the women on our last trip from the Conqueror?"

I knew from her shit-eating grin it'd be best to ignore her, but I couldn't help the question.

"What?" I asked, giving in. My curiosity would be the end of me one day.

"The Ivodians can *lick* with their dicks," she blurted out.

The next breath entered my lungs and stopped there. Shock blocked my throat.

Maddy looked at me like she'd just presented me with a birthday gift.

"What? How?" I finally exhaled.

"Well, you could find out exactly *how* this weekend." She shrugged, with that cruel, cruel smile still on her lips.

I blew a long breath out, staring at the control panel. All was fine with the instruments. Nothing required my urgent attention, allowing my thoughts to focus entirely on the commander... And now, on his *licking* dick, thanks to Maddy.

"What if he's a jerk in person?" I asked, blankly staring at the navigation display.

Maddy rolled her shoulders back.

"Well, he very well could be. Most men are jerks, except for my Jake, of course." She said the name of her fiancé with the same dreamy expression she always had when speaking about him.

Why couldn't I have fallen for a nice human guy, like Maddy did? Why did the alien commander of a freaking warship have to catch my attention?

I didn't know the answers to these questions, only that now that I knew the commander was out there, all other men had ceased to exist, human or alien.

"That's why you have to talk to him, to find out what kind of man he is. The commander could turn out to be very charming," Maddy said in a sing-song voice then added with a dramatic flair, "What if he's your soulmate? Your paths have crossed, but you'll let him slip away, not giving the two of you a chance. What then?"

"He's leaving soon, anyway." I shook my head. "Besides, there is no such thing as soulmates."

"Oh yeah? What about Jake and me, then?" She pinned me with a stare, challenging me to disagree..

I couldn't argue with that. Jake and Maddy were perfect for each other, a true match made in heaven. That could never be me and the commander, though, could it? We were people from literally different worlds.

Not that I was hoping to find a soulmate in the commander, anyway. Honestly, I wasn't sure what to expect, but I did wish for a chance to get to know him a little better. I didn't think I'd ever muster enough courage to ask him to spend the weekend with me. But I'd packed twice as many groceries to take with me to the cabin this afternoon. Just in case.

"Lori," Maddy said firmly. "The times when a woman sat in her parlor waiting for a man to notice her are gone. Today, women have the right to ask a man out. Use it, dammit."

I was running out of arguments.

The commander couldn't make the first move. He didn't know I existed, and he never would, unless I did something about it.

I released a sigh.

"Fine. Maybe I could come out briefly, just to say hi."

"And he'd say 'greetings,'" Maddy quipped. "And that would be the end of your conversation. You *have to* invite him to spend the weekend with you, or else it'll go nowhere."

I rubbed my forehead, my palms turning sweaty.

"I can't possibly go up to a man who's never seen me before and ask him to come to a remote cabin with me for an entire weekend."

"Why not?" Maddy looked at me innocently.

"Because no one does that. He'll think I'm an idiot," I said, exasperated.

"He's not from Earth, Lori. Remember? On Ivodi, apparently, men routinely come up to women they never saw before, grab them, and make them their wives. Trust me, your invitation wouldn't faze him. They have no women on the Conqueror. I'm sure he'd jump at the chance to have you all to himself for an entire weekend. Anyway, like I said, what do you have to lose? The Conqueror will leave the Earth's orbit soon, and you'll never see the commander ever again."

Never again.

That sounded devastating.

Chapter 3

Lori

"**G**o get him, tiger," Maddy growled, making a gesture with her hand as if it were a cat's paw with claws out.

I had her employee ID clipped to my chest. Her hat was sitting low on my forehead, partially hiding my face. I grabbed her tablet with the paperwork for today's passenger load and inhaled deeply, bracing myself.

"Why did I let you talk me into this?" I muttered under my breath.

"Yeah, you go, girl." She waved at me. "I'm not making you do anything you don't want to do."

That was true. I could blame it on Maddy all I wanted, but my heart's deepest desire for the past two weeks had been to at least exchange a couple of words with the Ivodian commander. All of this was my doing, now.

"Okay. You're in charge of the ship." I headed for the door.

My heart thundered so loud in my chest when I exited the shuttle, I was afraid I wouldn't be able to hear anyone over the echo of the heartbeat in my ears.

As usual, the Ivodians had already positioned themselves in a formation at the end of the docking deck, blocking the entrance from the deck to their ship—in case Maddy and I decided to storm it for any reason. As a military ship, they had their rules and protocols. One of them must be preventing the visitors from advancing inside the ship uninvited. They took it seriously, even if the potential threat was just two women armed with nothing but a taser.

"Greetings, First Officer Kwan." An Ivodian stepped forward, addressing me by Maddy's name and rank.

Maddy's guess proved correct. The Ivodian didn't spot that I was a different person. Judging by the bright purple insignia on the left sleeve of his white uniform, this was the deck supervisor.

I nodded, lowering the visor of my hat and lifting my tablet high to my eyes to hide more of my face. My heart kept thundering in my chest. My hands grew sweaty, threatening to let the tablet slip to the floor. I'd never broken a rule before, no matter how minor. I couldn't believe I was doing it now, and all because of this unstoppable desire to meet a man—one certain man who wouldn't leave my thoughts.

"Greetings." I kept my voice low, opening the first document I needed the deck supervisor to sign.

He pressed his thumb to the screen of my tablet, the print serving as his signature. I flipped it to the next document.

The women started showing up, accompanied by their abductors. Some women threw daggers with their glares at their escorts. Others held hands with their Ivodians, gazing at them tenderly. A team of counsellors waited for the women upon our landing in port. The specialists would hopefully help them sort out their feelings for the Ivodians.

Then the commander appeared, and I could no longer focus on anyone else.

I felt him approaching before I even saw him. The perfect formation of the Ivodians parted. The crew bowed their heads, giving him the Ivodian solute—two fingers of the right hand pressed to the top piercing in the row running vertically up the bridge of their noses to their foreheads.

The commander stepped out onto the dock and addressed the small group of human women.

"Ladies, it's been an honor having you on my ship. I wish you a safe journey home." His deep voice boomed under the high ceiling of the deck, reverberating through my chest and doing all kinds of things to my body.

My breath hitched when he strolled my way.

"Hi," I squeaked.

"Greetings." He inclined his head, touching a piercing on the bridge of his nose, the lowest one in the row.

There was a hierarchy assigned to their piercings, it appeared, and I must be on the lower end of it.

I met his dark-violet eyes rimmed with black and...went mute.

"Um..." was all I could manage, feeling like a teenager again, awkward and tongue-tied.

What was it about men that did this to me? I could work alongside them, be friends with them, but the moment I found a man attractive, I became this mumbling mess, unable to push a coherent word out.

Of course for some cruel reason, fate had made me fall for one of the most intimidating men in the Universe.

The commander towered over me, thick arms crossed over his wide chest. The pristine whiteness of his uniform was striking against the midnight purple of his skin. His piercings glimmered with silver. In addition to the row of crescents in the middle of his forehead, he also had three small thick hoops in each ear and a row of slim, white streaks embedded flat in the skin on either side of his bald head.

Like all Ivodians, his head wasn't perfectly round. His skull was slightly raised in the middle, forming a low ridge from his forehead all the way to the back of his head. Two smaller ridges protruded on each side, curving over his ears.

He stared at me from under his heavy brow for what appeared like an eternity. Lost in the deep violet of his eyes, I couldn't come up with a word to say, even if my life depended on it.

Again, I felt like I was back in high school crushing on the captain of our football team. After a full year of my pining over him, he'd finally spoken to me. Once. He'd asked to borrow my pencil sharpener in class.

I'd panicked and shoved it into his hands without a word, not even a smile. Needless to say, that remained my one and only interaction with the boy I'd dreamed about for a year.

I was not in high school anymore, dammit. I was turning thirty, for Pete's sake. My out-of-place shyness felt irritating and simply ridiculous.

Smoothing down my skirt with my sweaty hands, I raised my chin with determination.

"Commander!" My voice rang high with nerves. "Can I talk to you?"

He lifted an eyebrow ridge. A spark of interest in his eyes shaded by dark eyelashes sent a flock of shivers down my arms.

"In private..." I added breathlessly.

He flicked his gaze up and down my body. It didn't feel like leering. Maybe he was assessing me as a threat? Checking for anything I could possibly use as a weapon? I had nothing but the tablet. I hadn't even taken Maddy's taser with me.

"It won't take long," I assured him hurriedly, willing my heart to calm down, lest the commander hear it beat against my ribs.

To my relief, he nodded. Without asking any questions, he gestured at a silver metal door to the right.

"This way, please." His deep voice rumbled above me.

Trying not to swoon too much lest I pass out, I quickly turned to the deck supervisor.

"You can proceed with the boarding of the passengers. The captain will receive them," I told him, staying in the role of the first officer.

The deck supervisor headed over to the group of women waiting to get on the shuttle.

I had but a few moments to finally talk to the object of my affection. Clutching my tablet hard to stop my hands from trembling, I followed the commander through the silver door.

It appeared to be a storage room with long shelves on the walls and a screen terminal, probably to log in arrivals and cargo shipments, but maybe for something else entirely, for all I knew about Ivodian ship operations.

The commander stopped in the middle of the room. Turning to me, he stared at me expectantly.

"I'm listening." His deep voice softened, now that we were alone. He examined my face, the interest in his eyes growing deeper, more intense.

It got so hot, I almost panted for air. I wished I could pop open the top button of my shirt, but was afraid he'd take it as an invitation. Would it be good or bad if he did? I had no idea.

"My...my name is Lori," I started.

"Lori?"

His gaze flicked to Maddy's name badge clipped to my breast pocket, and my heart stilled. He lifted his hand, taking the badge between his fingers. His knuckles grazed my breast through my shirt and bra, sending a zap of desire through me. I closed my eyes, hoping he didn't notice my nipples standing to attention in response to his touch.

"Lori!" Maddy's voice sounded suddenly from behind the door.

What was she doing here? She was supposed to be boarding the women. Back on the shuttle.

The door slid open and Maddy barged in, pushing a cargo cart in front of her.

"What is this?" The commander frowned, slowly moving his hand away from me.

Maddy shifted her gaze between him and me.

"Um, these are suitcases." She shoved the cart aside. "For the women to pack their belongings."

Although most of the women had been abducted with nothing but the clothes they'd been wearing, the Ivodians had provided them with clothes and toiletries. Many of the abductors gave their "brides" gifts.

Some of the women also ordered things from Earth during the weeks they'd spent on the Conqueror. The Coalition of the Earth's Governments provided them with one piece of luggage for whatever belongings they wished to take from the ship with them.

"Lori, the base port called," Maddy said to me quickly. "I told them you were in the bathroom."

"Why?"

"Because…" she said slowly and with emphasis, making big eyes at me.

Because according to our contract with the Ivodians, I was supposed to stay with the ship. My employer wouldn't care that I'd stepped out unless the client complained about it. And there I was, standing right in front of the client, while breaking his rule.

The commander stepped closer. Oddly, he appeared rather pleased with having caught me. Finger under my chin, he lifted my face to his.

Breath caught in my throat. The awareness of his touch rushed me. He leaned so close to me, his scent reached my nostrils—warm, male, and otherworldly exotic. If I stood up on my tiptoes, I could kiss him.

His brow ridges moved closer together, deepening his frown. Kissing obviously wasn't on his mind.

"I'm detaining you for breaching the protocol," he said softly but firmly. "You have five minutes to request another crew from Earth to pick up your shuttle, Captain. You're staying on the Conqueror. Indefinitely."

I trembled from trepidation…and anticipation from his threat.

His threat…

He threatened me, not propositioned.

For Pete's sake, I had to get a grip!

He'd threatened to detain me. No matter how freaking sexy this man had proven to be up close, he was my company's client. If he complained, my career might be on the line.

I cleared my throat, stepping back from him.

"Allow me to explain, Commander—" I started, standing at attention.

A click sounded from behind me. The taser's prongs whizzed past me before embedding in the commander's neck.

"Maddy!" I gasped, realizing she'd finally seen the chance to use her taser—now, of all times. "What did you do?"

I whipped around to face her.

Looking even more shocked than me, Maddy clutched the taser with both hands.

The commander arched his back with a strangled growl. The wires in his neck buzzed with sparks. The look in his eyes promised murder to both of us.

"Shit," Maddy whimpered, pressing another button on her taser.

"Maddy, no!" I yelled in horror.

This time, a tranquilizer dart shot out, piercing the commander's skin next to the electric prongs.

"Maddy, stop it." I launched for her, but she pressed the trigger again, sending another shot of tranquilizer into the poor commander's neck.

"Why the hell doesn't he fall?" she squeezed through her teeth, with crazy determination on her face.

"Hey!" I grabbed her wrists, then pried the taser out of her stiff fingers. "It's not a video game. Do you hear me? Stop shooting him!"

The taser was useless anyway, now. All it'd had was an electric charge and two tranquilizer darts. It was designed to give the shooter a *choice* of means to neutralize the opponent, not to shoot the entire arsenal at once.

The double-dose of tranquilizer finally did it, though. The commander staggered, his hand going up to his neck. A moment later, he crashed to the floor.

"Fuck, Maddy, did you really have to do it?" I groaned.

"He said he'd arrest us," she said, scratching her head.

"What if you killed him?" I sank to my knees next to the commander and placed my hand on his neck. The pulse was still there, and his chest rose and fell with deep, even breathing. I exhaled in relief. "He's alive. For now, anyway. He needs medical attention." I made a move to get up, but Maddy placed her hand on my shoulder.

"He'll be fine," she said. "He'll just sleep for a few hours."

"How do you know?" My worry threatened to explode into panic.

"I had to take a course on how to use this thing, remember?" Maddy pointed at the taser I'd dropped on the floor.

"Did they teach you to fire everything you have into one person?" I asked sarcastically.

She had the decency to look ashamed.

"No. But I know even the whole thing isn't going to kill an Ivodian. These guys are like cyborgs, indestructible."

I hoped she was right. "We need to get someone in here, anyway."

"No. Wait." Maddy wildly roamed the room with her eyes. "We can't just walk out of here, with him lying like that. They'll kill us."

The Ivodians had proven to be an aggressive bunch who acted without asking. They'd aimed a whole bunch of weapons at Earth while they were grabbing our women off the streets.

"They won't kill us just for incapacitating him," I argued, with little conviction.

"What if they don't pause to investigate whether he's dead or alive? What if they shoot first and ask questions later?"

That was entirely possible.

"Kind of like you, right?" I couldn't help the sarcasm again, though Maddy's terrified expression tugged at my compassion.

"I'll be fired," she whimpered.

I stared at the motionless commander sprawled at our feet.

"More than just being fired, I'm afraid," I said.

At that point, losing our jobs seemed the least of what could happen to us.

"I'll be arrested and prosecuted if he presses charges," Maddy added in a small voice.

Me too, of course. I wasn't the one who pulled the trigger, but I was the captain in charge. All of it was my responsibility.

"Well, it's his prerogative to press charges, considering—" I started, but Maddy didn't let me finish.

"Listen," she whispered, grabbing on to my arm. "What if we don't tell anyone? Wait until he comes to instead, then talk to him? Privately. Maybe he is a nice guy, like you hoped, and he'll understand?"

Would the commander be understanding? He appeared to be very much a man of duty. And his duty in this case would be to report the incident to my superiors and make sure it was properly investigated.

At the same time, he'd been willing to step outside of the protocol and talk to me one-on-one before he'd spotted the wrong ID badge and Maddy had opened fire.

Maybe he would give me a minute or two to apologize and explain we meant no harm?

"We can't possibly sit here for hours waiting for the tranquilizers to wear off," I said.

"We could take him with us," Maddy suggested, with a wild look in her eyes.

"Where?"

"To Earth."

"Are you insane?" I gasped.

"But why not? You wanted to invite him to your cabin tomorrow, so take him." She pointed at the motionless commander on the floor, as if he were a loaf of bread in a supermarket, for me to take if I wished.

"That would be an abduction, Maddy, something we've been teaching the Ivodians not to do." I couldn't believe we were even talking about it.

"Right, but it's something *they've* done throughout their history," she argued passionately. "It's a part of their culture, Lori. He isn't human. He won't mind if you take him. He'd love it!"

"I'd be honored." I remembered the words of the first engineer when Felicity Davis had asked him how he would've liked to be the one abducted.

Maybe the commander wouldn't be too upset if I took him off the ship for a weekend? He might even welcome a break from his duties, a little getaway to see a part of Earth he'd never get to see otherwise. Maybe he truly would feel honored and flattered by my taking him. He might even be less angry and more willing to hear my apologies for this incident.

"Commander?" A male voice sounded suddenly, making both Maddy and me jump. "Second Engineer Khocak here. We need you on the bridge, please."

It took me a second to realize the voice was coming from the flat silver disk strapped to the commander's bicep. The disk was the Ivodians' communication device.

"We don't have much time," Maddy urged.

She was right. Time was pressing. The base port waited for me to take the call back on the shuttle. The Ivodians expected their commander to come out of this room any minute. The women had probably boarded on their own, ready to be taken back to Earth.

We had to act. Quickly.

I swept the room with my gaze, noticing another door opposite from the one we'd entered. The cargo cart that Maddy had wheeled in caught my attention next.

"Okay. Here is what we're going to do," I said, coming up with a plan as I went. "Unload the suitcases here."

Maddy snapped to attention, looking ready to jump into action. I slid the side doors of the rectangular cargo cart open and shoved the empty suitcases out while she stacked them on the nearest empty shelf.

Next, I unclipped the commander's communication device from his arm and crushed it under my foot. Sweeping the shards into the cargo cart to hide the evidence, I explained to shocked Maddy, "I don't know how to turn it off. If another call comes through while we're on our way back to the shuttle, it'll give us away."

She nodded in full agreement, being the true partner in crime that she was.

When the cargo cart was empty, I moved to the commander.

"Let's get him in, now."

The dead weight of the passed-out Ivodian proved not easy to maneuver. I hooked my hands under his arms and pulled up. My back strained. My knees shook. But all I managed was to lift his shoulders off the floor.

"Fuck, he weighs a ton," I hissed through my clenched teeth, lowering him back to the floor.

"It's the muscles." Maddy lifted the commander's leg to demonstrate his thick, well-toned thigh that his uniform pants couldn't hide. "See? Solid rock." She squeezed his leg.

"Okay, well… Let's not manhandle him more than necessary." I yanked his leg out of her hands.

"There has to be some serious *manhandling* involved if we want to get him in there." She tipped her chin at the open cargo cart.

Shaped like a long rectangular box, the cart was fully enclosed from all sides, which was perfect to hide the commander out of view. It was shorter than the Ivodian's tall body, however.

"Okay, fine. Just, you know, let's keep it to a minimum." I realized I was clutching his leg to my chest, rather possessively.

"Right." Maddy gave me a look. "Let's keep it to a minimum then, shall we?" She took the toe of the commander's boot between her thumb and her finger and removed his leg out of my arms.

"Let's try this." I slid the floor panel of the cart out.

Huffing and puffing, Maddy and I rolled the commander onto it with all his heavy bones and muscles. Then I made the panel slide back inside the cart, along with the commander.

"He'll need to travel with his knees bent," I said, seeing him crammed in there.

I adjusted his bent legs, hopefully making him more comfortable, then closed the cart.

"Well..." I exhaled sharply, blowing a few strands of my hair out of my face. "Get ready to leave, now."

Maddy grabbed her taser from the floor, winding up the wires back inside it.

I snuck to the door on the opposite wall. Pressing my ear to it, I made sure no sound came from behind it, then slid it open a little. A glance through the crack revealed a long, brightly lit corridor behind it.

"Perfect," I whispered, sliding the door close again. "We'll make them think he left this way."

Smoothing the skirt of my uniform over my thighs, I made sure my shirt was tucked in properly. I then adjusted my hat and traded our IDs and epaulettes back with Maddy.

"Ready?" I gave her a quick once-over. She looked frazzled, but passable. "I'll take this back to the shuttle." I grabbed the handle of the cart, shoving the tablet into her hands. "You finish up with the paperwork then do the walk-around as you usually do. And, you know... Act normal, okay?"

She nodded, obviously nervous.

I was nervous, too.

Squaring my shoulders, I slid the door open and stepped out and under the questioning gazes of at least a hundred Ivodians.

"Commander Nex was called to the bridge," I informed the desk supervisor, passing him by on my way back to the shuttle.

"Can I get your signature to confirm the delivery of the suitcases?" Maddy swept in with her tablet before the man managed to say a word of reply to me.

"What suitcases?" he asked, sounding confused.

"These ones." She waved her hand back at the luggage stacked in the room we'd just left.

Staring right in front of me, I kept moving along the docking deck toward the shuttle.

Opening the back doors, I slid the cart with the commander into the cargo bay under the cabin, then set the climate control to *live cargo* mode. Occasionally, we transported pets and other living creatures. The cargo hold was designed to accommodate them, allowing me to transport the commander if not in a very comfortable position, then at least in life-supporting conditions.

Sealing the cargo hold, I climbed inside the cockpit and finally took the call from Earth. Without using the word "diarrhea" outright, I devised a clumsy explanation for my delay in taking the call.

When Maddy climbed into her seat a few minutes later, I was able to exhale a full breath.

"All set?" I asked her, starting the sequence for take-off.

"I can't believe we did it." She stared at me, her dark eyes open wide.

This was just the beginning. I couldn't stop thinking about the commander cramped in the cart in the cargo hold.

What did I get myself into?

Chapter 4

Lori

"It'll be fine," Maddy reassured me once again, shortly before our re-entry into the Earth's atmosphere. "He'll come to, soon enough. You'll charm him, and you guys will have a lovely weekend together. A nice getaway for your birthday."

"Right, because 'Charm' is my middle name," I muttered under my breath.

"Well, it wouldn't hurt for you to be a little more approachable," she agreed. "Maybe this is a chance for you to practice that."

I shot her a glare. "Am I not approachable enough?"

She cast me a sideway glance.

"With that look on your face? Certainly not." She then added in a slightly warmer tone, "Lori, you clam up a lot, especially with the people you don't know. Remember, it took months of us flying together before you told me the story with your ex? The one about him stealing things and money from you?"

I heaved a sigh. Admittedly, I didn't have a very good track record with boyfriends. Of course, kidnapping a man now wasn't the best way to improve it, either. And Maddy was right, I wasn't a chatty type. I could fully be myself only with people I cared about and knew well.

"Just, you know, try to be charming when he wakes up," Maddy said. "Remember, we need his cooperation."

Charming? How the heck would one go about charming a man? An *alien* man, to boot? Especially since the commander didn't look very approachable himself.

I inhaled deeply, afraid I'd bitten off more than I could chew with this one.

"Do you want me to come with you?" Maddy asked with concern.

"Come where?" I blinked, snapping out of my uneasy thoughts.

"To the cabin. Are you worried he'll be angry when he wakes up? Are you afraid?"

"Afraid? No." I shook my head.

I felt sick to my stomach with worry, to the point that I feared my excuse about the diarrhea might become a reality soon. But I was not afraid for my life when I thought about being alone with the commander.

"After all, he threatened to have us arrested," Maddy reminded me.

"*Detained,*" I corrected. "He said 'detain.'"

"Same difference," she retorted.

There *was* a difference in the commander's word choice, though.

The memory of his finger sliding up my throat teased my skin with the phantom sensation of his touch. I remembered the spark in his violet eyes when he threatened to keep me on the Conqueror. He spoke to *me* when he said that—meaning me alone, not Maddy and me. Whatever it was he wanted to do to me, I believed it didn't involve authorities.

I didn't see Commander as a threat to my life and safety, even if he certainly didn't look harmless.

"I'm not afraid," I assured Maddy. "Besides, I'll be in my own cabin, on my property, in my world. I can take care of myself. You don't need to come. Didn't you have plans for this weekend, anyway?"

I remembered Jake getting some last-minute tickets to a show for the two of them after I'd adamantly refused to celebrate my birthday in the city.

"Yeah, the concert," Maddy dismissed with a flick of a wrist. "But I can always cancel it if you need my moral support in dealing with the grumpy Ivodian commander."

"No, don't cancel. You told me how happy Jake was about getting those tickets. You guys should go. I'll be fine. Promise. If worse comes to worst, I can always radio for help, remember?"

With no internet or cell service available at the cabin, radio was the only way to connect with the outside world from there. Not that I would need it, I hoped.

"Maybe he won't be grumpy when he's with you," Maddy speculated. "I'm sure he'll be happy to see that a woman like you cared enough to abduct him."

"I didn't *abduct* him," I protested. The word just didn't sound right. But was there any better word for what I was doing?

Maddy shrugged.

"Well, you *took* him, but whatever. The point is you are a smart, beautiful woman with a career. Any guy should be flattered to catch your attention."

That sounded way too close to what the first engineer had said to Felicity Davis when she was leaving him. He'd claimed that everyone should be proud to be his spouse. I did what had felt like the best thing to do in the situation at the time, but my taking the commander might be awfully close to an abduction, after all. Maybe even a kidnapping? Was there any real difference between the two? Was I a kidnapper now?

Dread trickled down my spine. For the hundredth time since the take-off, I wiped my sweaty hands on my skirt. I hoped when the commander woke up, he wouldn't be as upset as Felicity was about the abduction. I hoped he wouldn't stomp his feet and call me an asshole.

I hoped so much the situation still had a chance to resolve itself in some positive way.

UPON LANDING AT OUR base north of Toronto, I made sure the women disembarked safely, then helped them meet the group of the officials who were now in charge of them.

"Where's your plane?" Maddy asked when everyone was finally off the shuttle and off our hands.

I got my purse and jacket from the cockpit. It was a warm afternoon, typical for late June, but the nights were often chilly up north where I was going.

"In the hangar, like usual," I replied.

I loved my old Cessna. My parents bought it for me shortly after I'd started taking flying lessons. Owning an airplane turned out to be cheaper in the long run than renting one by the hour for my pilot training. I couldn't bring myself to part with it, even after I'd graduated college and got a job. Flying was also the most convenient way of getting to my grandpa's hunting cabin.

Maddy bit her lip, heading down the stairs to the tarmac. "We need to hurry."

We had minutes before the cleaning crew would come on board the shuttle. I absolutely had to get the commander out of the cargo hold before then.

"The luggage cart won't fit in your car." Maddy worried.

"It won't," I agreed. "I'll need to take him out."

She stared at me in shock.

"Right there in the parking lot? Are you crazy? Everyone will see that you're unloading an unconscious alien." She shook her head, heading to the door of the cargo hold. "We'll have to take my van. If we put the back seats down, the whole cart will fit."

"Now I'm stealing the cart, too?" After a nearly perfect career, my list of violations just kept growing today.

"Not stealing, borrowing." Maddy opened the door. "You'll bring it back on Tuesday, for our next flight. No one will even notice it was gone."

I heaved a sigh. In the grand scheme of things, what was stealing a luggage cart compared to stealing an alien commander? If I went to jail, it would be for the latter, not the former. At this point, I could take all the complementary soaps off the shuttle and the coffee machine, too. It wouldn't make it any worse.

"Fine." I rolled the cart out, then closed the door. "Let's just get out of here."

We rolled the cart to the employee parking lot. Working for a private company had the perks of more freedom and less control, as opposed to working for a government agency. Unlike airlines, space shuttle transportation was still relatively new and had fewer regulations and controls.

Maddy and I managed to squeeze the cart into her van only after we'd put all the seats down save for the driver's. Jamming it in there diagonally, we had just enough space to close the back door.

"I'll follow you." Maddy jumped in the driver's seat.

I ran over to my car. We made it to the hangar near the small airstrip where I kept my plane in less than forty minutes. Once there, I parked my car next to Maddy's van.

"How is he?" she asked when I opened the cart to check on the commander.

"Alive, thank goodness," I replied, touching his neck, then checking his breathing.

"Of course he's alive," she huffed. "But is he awake yet?"

"No." I stroked his head just above his ear. The daylight brought out the lighter tint of violet in the aubergine color of his skin. His eyes closed, the commander had a peaceful expression I'd never seen on his face before. In deep sleep, he didn't react to my touch. "You said he'd be out for a while."

"Right," Maddy replied. "That's what they said during the course I took."

"How long is 'a while' exactly?"

She shrugged. "I don't remember. Several hours? It was weeks ago. I just remember they insisted it was an effective method of neutralizing an Ivodian."

It'd been over three hours since the commander had been "neutralized." The flight to the cabin would take about three hours more.

"I'd love to move him into the seat," I said. "He'd be more comfortable, and it'd be safer to use the seatbelt."

Maddy waved at me with both hands. "Remember how heavy he is? We'll never be able to move him. Let's just keep him in the cart and put the whole thing in the back. Do you have something to strap the cart with?"

Locked in a cargo cart and strapped in the back was not how I envisioned taking the commander to my grandpa's cabin, on those few occasions when I'd allowed myself to dream about having actually asked him to come and him accepting my invitation.

Trailing my fingers down his bicep that stretched the long sleeve of his uniform, I had to agree with Maddy. Even if no one saw us here, the two of us couldn't physically move him.

"Once you get there, it shouldn't be long before he comes to," Maddy assured me.

I nodded, hoping the commander wouldn't wake up en route. He'd surely freak out then, finding himself cramped in a locked box.

After Maddy had given me a load of corny advice on how to "charm" a man, we said our goodbyes. I climbed in the pilot's seat of my single-engine airplane and rolled it out of the hangar.

I kept thinking about the commander cramped in the back of the plane the entire time we were in the air. For his sake, I hoped he'd sleep until I got him out of that box.

Chapter 5

Lori

It was late evening by the time I landed in the open field next to the cabin. I'd used the last light of the day to walk around the property to make sure everything was just the way I'd left it. In this isolated area, the possibility of a bear ransacking the place was a hundred times higher than having it burglarized by a person. Thankfully, all seemed fine.

From the shed just outside of the cabin, I grabbed a large rusty wheelbarrow I used to transport firewood. Then I wheeled the luggage cart out of the back of the plane and emptied it into the wheelbarrow. Still unconscious, the commander dropped in on his side, and I winced, hoping he didn't bruise anything.

Wheeling him into the main room of the one-bedroom cabin, I dumped him onto the couch. Hands on my knees, I bent over, panting to catch my breath. Either I was severely out of shape, or this man was a really heavy load.

He was alive and breathing, looking rather peaceful despite everything I'd put him through to get him here. His uniform was no longer the pristine white it used to be, though. The inside of the luggage cart proved to be dusty, leaving dark smears on the fabric along with some rusty stains from the wheelbarrow. There were also some small rips and tears on his knees and elbows. Thankfully, I didn't find any scratches on his skin. Apparently, the Ivodians' clothes were not as resilient as their men.

Sadly, I couldn't find anything in his size either from the clothes I stored in the cabin or from those I'd brought with me. The only thing in any way passable was a large navy Snuggie—a blanket that was also a...well, something with sleeves that one could wear, kind of.

Despite it being the end of June, the nights were pretty chilly. I covered the commander with the Snuggie, then went on to do the many things that needed to be done around the cabin before nightfall.

After taking the wheelbarrow back to the shed, I unloaded the large cooler and the bags of groceries I'd packed in the plane that morning. Despite all my hopes and plans, until that afternoon, I'd still believed I'd be spending this weekend alone. I'd doubted I would ever have the guts to ask the commander to join me here. And even if I'd mustered enough courage to ask, I hadn't thought he'd accept. Just in case, however, I had packed enough food for two people or even more, depending on how much Ivodian men ate.

Never in a million years had I expected a scenario that would end with the commander being tasered and tranquilized. Now, I waited for him to wake up with little patience and a lot of trepidation.

Night was approaching, I was hungry, and the commander was still deep asleep. I started the fire in the wood-burning stove, then distracted myself from anxious thoughts by making chili for dinner. When I had it simmering in the pot on the stove, a muffled groan came from the couch.

"Commander?" I hurried from the stove to the couch.

He sat up. The Snuggie slipped off his shoulders and pooled in his lap. He rubbed his neck, looking disoriented.

"Hi." I shifted foot to foot awkwardly, clutching the large wooden spoon I was using to stir the chili. "How are you feeling?"

Snapping his gaze to me, he leaped to his feet. Any trace of drowsiness disappeared from his posture and expression. His tails rose behind him menacingly, like whips ready to lash. Taking a wide stance and raising his fists, he appeared fully alert and ready to fight.

To fight *me?*

I squeaked, lifting the chili spoon in front of me as a weapon.

"You?" A flash of recognition was quickly replaced by disappointment in his eyes. It cut me like a knife. "Are you alone, Captain? Where am I?" His eyes roamed the interior of the cabin—dark log walls, a thick support beam under the ceiling, a kitchen area behind me and the door to the one and only bedroom to the right of us.

The yellow checkered couch he'd slept on was the biggest piece of furniture in the room. Grandma's knitted cushions were tangled with my Snuggie on it.

"It's my hunting cabin," I said, keeping the spoon between us, just in case, as he remained in his ready-to-fight pose.

"Hunting?" he looked confused now.

"Yes. It's...um, a getaway," I mumbled. The whole idea of bringing him here sounded so ridiculously stupid now. "It's my birthday tomorrow," I added, hoping in desperation he might take it easy on a birthday girl.

He glowered at me. His tails remained suspended in the air behind him, and I wondered if he could really whip an opponent with them. Dark and thin, they looked very much like the cords of a cat o' nine tails, spread through the air like a fan.

"Where is this *cabin* located?" he demanded.

"Where? You mean geographically?"

"Yes. Show me on the map." He pointed at my cell phone on the kitchen table.

I scratched my ear.

"Yeah, no, that thing is useless around here. We're in one of the few places on Earth with no service, at all."

He gave me a suspicious look, one that made me feel so small, I feared I might fall through the cracks in the floor and stay there. Maybe it'd be better if I did.

"Okay, just wait a moment." I carefully stepped around him on my way to the basket by the door where I stored odds and ends. I pulled out an old laminated paper map from the basket. "This one is super outdated, but it'll give you a general idea of our location."

I spread the map on the table made from thick wood, its surface unfinished but polished by use over time. He craned his neck to see the map, keeping his distance from me.

"We're here." I pointed at the light green spot of the open field in front of the cabin in the sea of the dark green of the forest on the map. "The only way to get to the cabin by road would be through here." I traced with a finger a curved dotted line that snaked between the patches of green. "The road is pretty rough and windy, though. You'd need a good vehicle and a couple of days. We came by plane today."

He stared at the map, his gaze following my finger.

"Why am I here?" Arms crossed over his chest, he took an imposing stance. At least he'd abandoned the fighting pose. Though, I didn't doubt the commander could launch an attack from any position.

I drew in a breath, pondering the best way to explain what had happened.

"It was an accident... Kind of. A misunderstanding."

He lifted one of his heavy brow ridges, looking extremely skeptical.

"You work for the Coalition of Earth's Governments," he stated flatly. "I have complied with the Coalition's demands. What do you want, now? A ransom?"

I blinked at him, lost for a moment. What the heck was he talking about? Maybe there had been more than just tranquilizers in those shots? Or did he bump his head in the luggage cart on the way here? Which was entirely possible.

"Commander, you know I work for Starlight Spacelines. I fly the shuttle to your ship three times a week. And no, I don't want a ransom. I'm not a kidnapper." I winced.

So far, my actions had been very much in line with those of a kidnapper. I groaned inside. This was not the way I'd dreamed about finally having a conversation with the commander. I hadn't planned to kidnap him. The most I'd ever hoped for was to have a talk, then maybe, maybe the pleasure of his company this weekend, which obviously didn't promise much pleasure at all now.

"I swear, I didn't plan for it to happen this way," I said. "I'm very sorry for having whisked you away like that. It seemed like the best solution at the time, considering the circumstances. However..." I blew out a breath. "I'll take you back to the city, first thing tomorrow morning."

It was the only right thing to do. Despite what the first engineer had said, the commander definitely didn't look "honored" by my abducting him.

"You'll find someone to take me back, right now," he bit off in a voice so hard it could probably cut metal. It didn't help that the heavy eyebrow ridges over his eyes gave him a perpetually grumpy expression.

As angry and scary as he looked, I shook my head.

"There is no one else around here. I'm the only one who can fly you back. But it's dark out there, and the wind has picked up significantly. I'm also tired after the crazy day I've had. It'd be much safer to fly tomorrow."

"Were you the one who flew us here?" He cocked his head. I could almost see the thoughts processing in his head. The expression in his eyes remained sharp, calculating.

"Yes, I'm a pilot, remember? I can fly other craft, not just the space shuttle."

He gave me a measuring stare, sliding it down my body. I shifted from foot to foot again, suddenly feeling self-conscious in my cozy sweatshirt, comfy jeans, and fuzzy fur slippers.

"What kind of a pilot are you if you can't fly at night?" he asked.

My blood heated, urging me to lash out. I counted to ten to calm down before replying evenly enough.

"A cautious pilot lives longer. I have no landing strip, no lights here. If I were stupid enough to fly before the sunrise, we'd risk crashing on take-off."

He ran his fingers over the rows of implants on the left side of his head.

"Is this place yours?" he asked out of the blue.

"Yes. I own it."

"By yourself?" He took his hand away from the implants. "You live here alone?"

"Yes. It's my hunting cabin. I come here for holidays. Why?"

His expression grew darker. His jaw ticked.

"Is there no one else who could fly me? I need to get back, now," he said with force.

"No, there is no one else," I repeated again. He must have bumped his head since he just didn't seem to get it. "*Now* is not going to happen—"

He hurled me a glare like a dagger, cutting me off. The mighty commander obviously wasn't used to people arguing with him.

"I need to be back on my ship!" he snapped so loud, it made me jump.

"You see?" I pointed with my spoon at him. "That's why abductions don't work. You can't pluck people out of their lives and expect them to be okay with that. It doesn't feel so good to be abducted, does it?"

Something flashed in his eyes, something that looked incredibly like fear.

"You *abducted* me." His voice came out hollow. He absolutely didn't seem pleased or flattered about my "choosing" him.

"Technically..." I bit my lip before continuing carefully, "...it looks like I kind of did. I'm sorry. It wasn't my intention, please believe me."

With a long rush of air from his lungs, he plopped back on the couch. I finally felt safe enough to lower my spoon—at this point, he looked deflated rather than aggressive.

"I'm sorry," I said softly, gutted by his crestfallen expression. "It was an accident. Maddy overreacted, and I lost control of the situation. As the captain, I assume full responsibility—"

He glared at me again. I had every reason to believe he was genuinely pissed.

"You wore a wrong ID," he stated accusingly.

So much for the belief that all humans looked the same to the Ivodians. The commander had figured out who I was fairly quickly. I heaved a long breath.

"I did," I confessed.

"Why?"

"I..." God, this was going to sound so awfully stupid. "I just wanted to have a chance to speak with you."

His eyelids dropped a little, but didn't hide the now-familiar spark of interest in his eyes that I'd first spotted back on the Conqueror. The commander might hate me, but he was also curious about me.

"To speak, you could've contacted me through the central communication system," he said rather calmly.

I could have, but that would involve filing a request through the Ivodian Security Team and then having our conversation recorded.

"I wanted to speak face-to-face. In private."

The spark in his eyes burned hotter now, even as he narrowed his eyes with suspicion.

"Why?" he asked in that deep voice of his, stretching the word slowly as if it were a piece of soft caramel.

I twisted the spoon in my hands, feeling my face heating under his stare. Most people blushed less as they grew older. However, my face seemed to burn with more intensity than ever. It must be the effect the commander had on me.

"It wasn't an official matter," I mumbled in reply. "I just wanted to..."

"I wanted to know what kind of a person you were..."

"I love hearing your voice, even if it's thundering with anger as it was just minutes ago..."

"I hoped to learn more about you..."

"I wondered if you'd like to get to know me, too..."

Faced with his stern expression, none of the answers seemed right, no matter how true they were. Saying nothing, I dropped my gaze down, fidgeting with the spoon in my hands.

He obviously wasn't pleased to be here with me. For Ivodians, the act of abduction might be akin to a marriage proposal, an invitation to a romantic relationship. It was safe to say the commander didn't accept my invitation.

"Why did you want to talk to me, Lori?" his voice softened even more.

He remembered my name, at least.

"It's not important anymore." I waved him off with the chili spoon.

What difference would it make if I told him the truth? He clearly didn't want to be here with me. If I confessed that deep in my heart I'd hoped for a romantic weekend together, it would only make me look desperate and pathetic at this point.

"You know," I said instead. "The dinner should be ready by now. Let's eat, then we'll get some sleep. You can have the bedroom. I'll take the couch. First thing after breakfast tomorrow, I'll fly you back to the city. Okay?"

A muscle in his jaw moved again. He pressed his mouth into a firm line.

"Is there really no one else who could take me back?" he asked.

Dammit, I didn't know he despised me *this* much—he didn't even want to sit in the plane for a few hours with me. Or maybe it had something to do with his less than stellar opinion about my flying skills. Either way, the hurt churned in my chest.

"Do you see anyone else around?" I spread my arms wide in the invitation to search for another pilot in a hundred-mile radius or more. "Sorry, there isn't. I am the only one who can fly you out of here, and I'll do it in the morning. Our next shuttle to your ship is on Tuesday. I'll pay for your hotel until then," I added, feeling responsible for inconveniencing him. "Or you can call your buddies to pick you up. Either way, I'm sorry for the inconvenience but you will have to spend the night here."

Avoiding his gaze, I moved to the stove with the cast-iron pot of chili bubbling on it.

By now, I was really starving. The commander must be hungry, too. Hungry people generally tended to be angrier. Maybe if we ate, we'd be able to talk without this awkward tension hanging over us. Well, it was awkward on my part. The cloud of tension that hung over the commander would be much darker and crackling with rage.

I spooned the chili into two hand-painted ceramic bowls and cut up the loaf of bread I'd brought from the city. I had packed a bottle of wine, too. Chili went great with a glass of red wine, in my opinion. Seeing the commander's grim expression, however, I decided not to mention the wine. This wasn't a date, after all, not even close. Instead of wine, I got two bottles of water from the cooler box and set them on the table next to the bowls of chili.

"Lori."

I jumped as the commander's heavy hand landed on my shoulder.

When I turned, his stern gaze met mine. How did he manage to sneak up on me so quietly? A man his size shouldn't be able to move around this room without bumping into furniture that crowded it. His massive chest alone could create whirlwinds in his wake, I imagined.

"Lori," he repeated as I stared at him expectantly. "No one, I mean absolutely no one, can know about you taking me off the Conqueror. Ever," he added with emphasis. "Understood?"

The intensity in his voice made me pause.

"Well, I'm... It's not exactly in my interests to tell anyone. I actually wanted to ask *you* not to file a report about the incident. Unlike Ivodians, neither my bosses nor our government would take lightly my abducting you."

He winced at the last sentence, not easing his grip on my shoulder.

"I need you to give me your promise," he demanded.

"Sure." I felt confused and slightly intimidated by his adamant request. "I promise I'll never tell anyone about this. If you keep it a secret, too, no one will ever know." I then added, "Except for Maddy."

"Maddy?" His forehead furrowed even more. "Is that the first officer?"

I nodded. "Yes. But don't worry, she won't say a word."

"How much do you trust her?"

"A lot. Maddy is an excellent pilot and a responsible employee, generally. She made a mistake by tasering you, but we all make mistakes, don't we?" Admittedly, not all of them ended with a man lying unconscious on the floor. "She's been a very good friend, too. She won't tell anyone," I assured him.

As the one who pulled the trigger, Maddy sure wasn't interested in broadcasting it anywhere. We'd wanted to get the commander away from his ship and his crew, so that when he woke up, I could talk him into not reporting us. That proved easier than we'd thought, despite my complete and utter inability to "charm" him. Apparently, he didn't want to make the incident public, either.

At least there was one thing we appeared to be in agreement about. I exhaled in relief. Seemingly satisfied with my answer, too, he finally let go of my shoulder.

I took a look at his ruined uniform.

"Sorry about your clothes," I said, guilt rising inside me about the less-than-comfortable way I'd made him travel here. "If you take it off, I can wash—"

"I'm not disrobing, human," he barked, cutting me off.

Great. Now, he probably thought I was dying to see him naked. I'd just become a pervert in addition to a kidnapper in his eyes.

I lifted both hands in the air in a placating gesture.

"Suit yourself. I just wanted to help. Trust me, it's not a ploy on my part to get you naked."

Wouldn't that be exactly what a pervert would say? I pressed my lips firmly together. Maybe it'd be best for me to just stay quiet for a little while.

The commander growled something incomprehensible under his breath then focused his attention on the food on the table. Not waiting for another invitation, he shoved a chair back from the table then plopped in it, making the poor piece of furniture groan under his weight.

"Did you make it yourself?" He pulled a bowl of chili closer, eyeing it suspiciously.

I sat on the chair across from him.

"Yes, it's my grandma's old recipe," I said, glad to finally have a safe topic for a conversation. "She always added bacon and used whole cloves of garlic. Try it, people usually like it."

He sniffed the steam rising over the bowl, then picked up his spoon.

"And this?" He pointed at the plate of shredded cheddar cheese I placed in the middle of the table.

"It's cheese." I sprinkled some in my bowl. "You put it on top."

He watched me take a spoonful of chili in my mouth and waited until I swallowed.

"Commander, I'm not trying to poison you." I rolled my eyes. "I've had a million chances to hurt you in the past few hours while you were unconscious. Trust me, I mean no harm."

He tossed me another one of his suspicious glares but ended up taking a spoonful of the chili, too.

I tried to guess by his expression what he thought about the dish. This was a freaking good chili. Everyone who'd tried it loved it. With the Ivodian, however, I had no idea what to expect.

"Here is some salt and pepper if you need to add." I slid the two shakers over the table to him.

He took both, sprinkled some from each into his wide palm, then licked it off. I noticed his dark-red tongue was forked at the tip—something I didn't know about the Ivodians. How could I? None of them had shown me their tongues before.

The commander unscrewed the top of the pepper shaker, then dumped one third of its contents into his chili bowl.

"Um..." I made a move to stop him, but failed to do so in time.

"What?" he glanced at me.

"It may be just a tad too much," I warned.

He swirled his spoon in the chili, mixing the pepper and the cheese in, then took a huge spoonful of it in his mouth.

I cringed inside, expecting him to spit it out right away.

"Holy Serpent of Ahell," he groaned, a blissful expression spreading on his normally stern face. "This is probably the best food in the entire Universe."

"Really? You think so?" My face heated with pleasure from his praise. My heart bit faster.

"Did you really make it all by yourself?" He kept shoving the chili in his mouth by huge spoonfuls.

"Do you see any kitchen staff around?" I quipped, my mood lightening. "I don't need help to cook chili. Or anything, really. I like cooking."

He peered at me over another spoonful of chili.

"A pilot who can cook." He shook his head. "Human women never cease to amaze me."

It wasn't clear whether he was pleased or disturbed by the fact that a woman could do both cooking and flying. It did sound kind of like a compliment, though. Sadly, I never knew how to properly receive a compliment.

I shrugged awkwardly. "Do Ivodian women cook?"

"They do. All of them," he said confidently, as if he had personally tested the cooking skills of each woman on his planet. "None know how to operate an aircraft, though."

He finished the chili, licked the spoon, then stared forlornly into the empty bowl.

"What stops your women from learning how to fly a plane?" I asked, getting up.

"It's just not done."

I refilled his bowl with more chili. He added the cheese and the ungodly amount of black pepper then dug in eagerly.

"Things change," I said, taking my place at the table again. "Just because it hasn't been done doesn't mean it couldn't be explored."

He shook his head resolutely.

"Women are rare on Ivodi. Female fetuses are less likely to survive a pregnancy, and many female babies don't even make it to a full month of life."

"That's awful," I gasped. "Why?"

"Women are a weaker sex, much more susceptible to illnesses and infections," he said as a mater-of-fact.

It was tragic that nature had dealt the women of his planet an unfair hand, especially considering how exceptionally resilient the Ivodian men were.

"I'm so sorry to hear that. I never knew," I said, softly.

"Those who do survive are cherished and treasured," he continued. "An Ivodian woman would never be allowed to hold an occupation where there is any risk to her health involved. Our women don't operate heavy machinery. They don't drive, don't fly, don't lift anything heavy. They travel in climate-controlled vehicles and are always accompanied by their husband or a male relative if they have to leave the house."

"I see." That would feel confining to me personally, but I understood the reasons for that in his culture.

He finished the second bowl of chili in a blink of an eye, then thoroughly licked the spoon.

"This is by far the best Earth food I've ever tried."

He leaned back. His stern expression smoothed.

Feeding him had been a good decision.

"Thank you." I allowed myself a smug smile. I knew my chili was good. "What other Earth foods have you tasted?"

"A few. Some were better than others but all lacked spice."

"Of course!" I laughed. "No one would think about adding half a shaker of pepper in a dish." I took a mental note to refill it right after dinner.

"Why not?" He lifted the pepper shaker to his nose and inhaled deeply. "This is one good spice to have."

His nose wrinkled, shifting the piercings on its bridge closer to each other. His eyebrow ridges crawled up his forehead as his eyes grew bigger. A loud sneeze erupted from him, making the old glass windows in the cabin rattle and the dishes on the table shake.

I jumped, momentarily deafened by the sound, then laughed.

"Bless you!" I managed to say between bouts of laughter. "The pepper would do it to you. It makes you sneeze."

He stared at me, something akin to a smile curving up the corners of his shapely mouth.

"Like I said, good spice."

Chapter 6

Commander

The female went to bed shortly after dinner. He knew her name, but resisted using it. Referring to her as simply "the female" in his mind felt safer. He couldn't let her get too close, not even in his mind.

She'd wanted him to sleep in the small bedroom off the main area of her rustic dwelling, but he'd refused. The bedroom had only one window, too small for him to fit through to escape.

And he absolutely had to escape.

He liked her adorable laugh and amazing cooking. Dammit, he liked everything about that woman. But he couldn't allow any of it to lure him or impair his judgement. It was best to think about her as the Coalition's spy, which she very well could be.

When he'd first realized that the Earth shuttle was manned by an all-female crew, he found it unusual but not alarming. He felt intrigued, studying the first officer as she fluttered around his docking deck, organizing the passengers and doing the exterior inspection of the shuttle before each take-off.

He'd also caught a few glimpses of the captain through the windshield of their craft. She was elusive, remaining on board as he had requested in the contract. He'd put that clause in, not wishing the human crew to roam all over his deck. Had he known the crew would comprise two young attractive females, he would've thought twice before putting it in.

The first officer was lovely, but she wore a ring on the finger that signified she'd been claimed by a man already. Ivodians didn't get involved with the women already taken. Besides, she appeared too outgoing for his tastes.

As soon as the captain had approached him, however, blushing and tripping over her words, something primal stirred in him. He didn't care that she held a position of authority herself. He wanted to grab her, lock her in his bedroom, and protect her from the world.

He would've done just that had the meddlesome first officer not intervened with her taser.

Now, he worried his little shuttle captain might not be what she seemed. She never explained why she brought him here or what she had so urgently wanted to discuss with him back on the Conqueror. He suspected it was just a ruse to take him off the ship.

She worked for Starlight Spacelines, which had been contracted by the Coalition of the Earth's Governments, the same organization that had secretly detained his Second-in-Command. Officer Urrex had been held prisoner for two weeks now, as collateral to ensure the release of all human women from the Conqueror.

The Coalition had captured his Second-in-Command, then demanded a return of every single female his people had abducted. They had forced him to comply, knowing an Ivodian would never give up on one of their own.

He'd had no choice but to release the women. Now, he wondered if the Coalition had somehow gotten word about what he planned to do next.

He had released the human females to appease the Coalition and get his Second-in-Command back. That didn't mean the crew of the Conqueror would leave Earth's orbit empty-handed.

The Ivodian warriors never retreated in defeat. For the past decade that he'd been their commander, the crew had successfully completed every single mission they had undertaken. And he was not going to change that.

They'd come here to obtain brides for the ninety-seven of his warriors who had earned the privilege to retire from the ship. The excitement and anticipation among his crew had hit high when they got the word from Ivodi that the females of the newly discovered planet Earth had proven to be physically and biologically compatible with Ivodians. With just a minimal medical intervention, even breeding with them was possible.

He had given his men his word that they would have what they'd come here for. And no one, not even the exceptionally appealing human female sent by the Coalition, would make him go back on that word.

Once the last abducted woman was released from the Conqueror and Officer Urrex was back on board, safe and sound, the crew would grab ninety-seven females of child-bearing age and fight anyone who would try to stop them.

He needed to get back to his ship as soon as possible. But it couldn't be the human female who flew him there. Since she was the one who had taken him off the ship, he couldn't be seen in her presence. He needed to get back on his own.

In the pale light of the Earth's Moon filtering through the windows of the primitive dwelling, he found the map the female had shown to him. Carefully examining it, he gathered that his current location was in the Northern hemisphere of the planet.

He searched his memory for the information he studied about the Earth on their way here. The planet generally had few deadly predators. None of them were large enough to be considered a serious threat for an Ivodian male. The majority of the poisonous serpents and insects inhabited warmer climates. This part of the Earth was as safe as a planet could be. The biggest danger he'd face on a long hike would be just getting tired.

According to the map, it would take him almost three days on foot to reach the closest town. All he had to do to reach it was to follow a river.

He had once crossed the sands of the largest desert on the planet Eercu, populated with the deadliest giant centipedes known to the Universe. He had successfully combatted the nightmarish serpents of Hiveas, whose touch could result in a flesh-eating disease and whose bite would instantly kill a man. He had survived for nine days on the mountains of molten lava of the planet Phoruh, equipped only with a portable emergency shelter and a small flask of water. A three-day hike through the picturesque landscape of the Northern hemisphere of Earth promised to be an easy, pleasant stroll compared to what he'd been through in his life.

Searching through the cabin, he gathered whatever supplies he thought might be helpful on this journey. He found a primitive gas-fueled lighter to start a fire. Since the female had spoken about high winds, which could mean cool nights, he decided to take the funny blanket with sleeves she'd left on the couch for him. His uniform was too thin and held no warmth, designed for the climate-controlled interior of a spaceship.

A weapon was always handy, even in the non-hostile territory like this one. So, he took the knife in a worn leather sheath he found lying on the shelf by the door.

He would have plenty of drinking water available since his route lay along a river, but he didn't know how safe the water was to drink. It was best to boil it. So, he took a small pot from the shelf over the stove and a couple of bottles of drinking water from the cooler box, for convenience.

A container with the leftover dinner caught his attention when he was about to close the cooler box, and he grabbed it, too. The food the female had made was the best he'd had since arriving on this planet, and he couldn't resist taking the leftovers.

At the exit, he paused, casting a glance back at the bedroom door. Lori was sleeping in the room behind it.

He knew he shouldn't allow himself to wonder whether she slept naked or wearing some adorable fuzzy pajamas that went with her pink furry slippers. He had no business imagining how warm and cozy she would be snuggled under her blankets, her long, wavy hair spread over the pillow, her gray-blue eyes closed in slumber. He had to clear his memory of her sweet feminine scent he'd caught back on the Conqueror, of her smile and the sound of her laughter. He shouldn't be imagining how her skin felt to the touch, how her lips tasted, or how pliable her body would be if he bound her with his tails.

His cock most certainly had no right getting hard and achy when he thought of her. He must train himself to think of her as a possible spy for the Coalition and the woman who dishonored him by abducting him from his own ship. By doing so, she'd put in jeopardy everything he'd worked for so hard.

Opening the front door as noiselessly as possible, he slipped out into the night.

The air was cool, but nothing he couldn't handle, even when wearing the flimsy indoor uniform he had on. Tossing the bundle with his supplies over his shoulder, he headed toward the sound of water rolling over the rocks. Once he'd reached the riverbank, he headed west, along the current.

A high-pitched noise buzzed in his ear, annoying but too soft to be threatening. He waved it off. Something stung his head, and he slapped the spot. It must be an insect. He was certain the insect wasn't venomous—there weren't that many dangerous insects this far up North—its bite wouldn't be lethal. His skin just itched a little after its sting. He rubbed at it to alleviate the itch. Another sting pricked the back of his neck, and he scratched that spot, too.

His vision, superior to humans', made finding his way in the dark relatively easy. The calm of the night allowed him to let his guard down somewhat and enjoy the scenery. The woody, rocky landscape reminded him of the plot of land he had recently been approved to buy by the government of Ivodi.

After proving themselves in service on a warship, Ivodian warriors earned an honorary retirement that came with a choice of a permanent place of residence and a generous monetary allowance for life.

He'd selected a beautiful estate—not a farm, for he knew nothing about farming, and not a seashore, but a mountainous property in the lush forest of Us'ae, one of Rimall's three moons.

The Council had long approved him for a wife, too. He could retire anytime. At thirty-eight, he was certainly in the age range when many warriors chose to end their service on the ship, abduct a wife, and settle down. However, he believed he still had a few years of service and a few missions in him before he'd pass the leadership of the Conqueror on to another deserving male. He was not ready to retire yet.

For that reason, he hadn't thought too much about his future wife before. Now, he wished she'd have long, dark, wavy hair.

Like Lori...

He tripped over a clump of grass when the thought of her barged into his mind again, then scratched the spot of another insect sting right above his ear.

Now that he was a safe distance away from Lori and her cabin, he could allow himself to think about her beautiful hair, couldn't he? Ivodians had no hair. And he never cared for it before. But now... He wished he would've at least found a pretense to touch it once. But when?

Maybe at dinner? Changed out of her uniform, Lori appeared younger and as vulnerable as any Ivodian woman. Yet she seemed to do well on her own, even in that primitive dwelling of hers.

When his men did their final round of abductions before leaving this planet, he had to make sure none of them would snatch Lori. He couldn't have her for himself, but the possibility of her ending up in another male's bedroom made his skin crawl and his stomach twist in knots with a feeling he couldn't name.

His chest vibrated with possessive growls, and he kicked a rock in his path hard enough to make it splash into the stream.

If he couldn't have Lori, no one would.

And he could *not* have her.

After he'd so stupidly let himself be abducted, he couldn't even be seen with her anywhere. His crew would question him being in the middle of nowhere, one-on-one with a human female, on her property.

They might already be searching for him, and he couldn't allow them to find him anywhere near her. If word of him being fooled and taken by a female came out, he'd lose the respect of his men. If that happened, he'd not only be voted down from his position as their leader, he'd have to say goodbye to all benefits that he'd earned during his entire career. More than that, he'd be ridiculed by every Ivodian for the rest of his days.

Abductions of females had been a part of the Ivodian culture since the beginning of time. No female had ever taken a male before.

He'd be damned if he became known as the first male who got abducted by a woman.

Chapter 7

Lori

"Well, happy birthday, Lori." I smiled, talking to myself.

There was no one else to say that to me because for the longest time, I'd planned to spend this day alone. It was my first birthday since Grandpa was gone. He died in the hospital, exactly one year ago, on my twenty-ninth birthday, and today would forever be bittersweet for me.

My grandparents and I had been very close. As a kid, I'd spent every summer here, in the cabin with them, while my mom and dad worked in the city. Grandma showed me how to cook, and grandpa taught me everything about these woods—how to hunt and fish and how to survive in the wilderness.

For a while, I'd been looking forward to having a peaceful weekend on my own. Except that right now, I had the pissed-off Ivodian commander sleeping on my couch.

He'd need breakfast. From what I'd learned about the man so far, it was best to keep him fed. He became slightly more agreeable with his belly full.

The man had reasons to be grumpy, of course, I didn't blame him. Personally, I'd be just as upset if someone I didn't know snatched me and flew me across the province without asking for my permission.

All I could do now was to make him a big breakfast and fly him back, just like I'd promised. We'd started off wrong, but maybe we could at least part amicably.

Climbing out of bed, I put on some comfy clothes—a blue checkered shirt and a pair of jeans—then waddled sleepily into the main living room.

The couch was empty. Commander Nex and my Snuggie were gone.

"Commander?" I called, rubbing my eyes. "Commander Nex?"

I turned around, wondering where he could be. There simply was no place for someone his size to hide inside the cabin.

Did he go outside to pee, maybe? Needing to use the outhouse myself, I stomped out onto the log step in front of the entrance.

The commander wasn't anywhere outside where I could see. The outhouse also proved to be unoccupied. I searched the nearby area, calling him by his rank out loud, with no reply.

Worry creeped in. What could've happened to him? He couldn't have just evaporated into thin air.

Crouching by the wide log that served as a step at the threshold of the cabin, I inspected the ground carefully.

The commander's footprints were hard to miss. The soles of his boots had a distinct traction pattern. Due to his weight, the imprints were also deep and clear in the grassless dirt in front of the entrance. From the appearance of his footprints, he hadn't been dragged out of the cabin or running in fear.

He'd just...walked away.

I sat on the step, my legs refusing to support me. It wasn't easy to accept that a man would rather run into the woods at night, risking being attacked by bears and cougars, than spend a few hours under the same roof with me.

My self-esteem couldn't take that easily. What woman's could?

From the moment he'd dropped to the floor in the storage room on the Conqueror, the darts and taser prongs sticking out of his neck, there'd been little chance for anything real ever happening between us.

I'd still hoped we could part on good terms, though. I'd promised to fly him back this morning, and I had fully intended to keep my promise.

Why did he leave? Did he not believe me? Did he think I'd hold him here against his will or something? I must've left an even worse first impression than I'd feared.

But *where* was he going?

My concern for the commander grew. This was one of the very few remote places left on the planet. People unfamiliar with the area ran a huge risk when wandering off on their own. He could easily get lost.

Worry pounding in my head, I ran back to the cabin. Taking a quick walk around, I noted what was missing—my hunting knife, the container with the leftover chili, the laminated paper map, and...the Snuggie.

So, I now had a wrapped in a Snuggie alien roaming the wilderness armed only with a knife and with enough food to last him for a few hours at best.

He didn't stand a chance out there. I had to find him.

Grabbing my hunting backpack off the hook, I checked its contents, making sure I had the necessities there—a flashlight, dry matches, my Swiss Army knife, and a compass, along with other things that made hiking and camping in the wilderness survivable, like a first aid kit and a fishing line and lure. Then, I packed food and water, bug spray, my sleeping bag, and the lightweight three-person tent that rolled into a pack just slightly bigger than my fist.

Finally, I took my grandpa's rifle out of the locked gun box where I stored it. I still used it about once a year for hunting with a small group of friends who enjoyed the wilderness as much as I did.

I'd once brought a guy I was dating here, a city boy. He'd lasted for less than a day before begging me to take him back to his apartment in the city with indoor plumbing, Netflix, and a microwave.

How long would an alien last in the Canadian wilderness? An alien who'd spent his life traveling through space in a high-tech ship equipped with the latest, state-of-the-art amenities?

Concern for the commander had been steadily increasing, filling me with anxiety. I'd been hunting in these woods since I was six, first with my grandpa and later on my own. But even I wouldn't go out there alone in the middle of the night unless I had a damn good reason to do so.

Was running away from me a good reason to risk his life?

I shoved that thought aside. First, I needed to find him, hopefully safe and sound. Then I'd have enough time to deal with the damage this whole ordeal had done to my ego.

After lacing up my hiking boots, I heaved my backpack up and slung the rifle over my shoulder.

Praying I wasn't too late, I headed off into the woods.

THE COMMANDER WASN'T hard to track. The distinct soles of his boots left clearly identifiable prints in the dirt and deep indents in the areas covered with moss, grass, or pine needles. In addition, he left a path of snapped off twigs and branches in his wake wherever he'd barged through the underbrush.

He either had no idea how to move through the woods without leaving a trail or simply didn't care if I followed him. Either way, he appeared to be making quick progress along the river, though I still had no idea what destination he had in mind. There was nothing around here, nothing that could be reached on foot in a reasonable time. He was heading away from the only place that would give him shelter and transportation back to the city—my cabin.

His actions made no sense.

By midday, I finally came upon the place where the commander had taken a break. I was pleased to discover he'd made a fire. He seemed to know what he was doing, too, which was a relief. The fireside appeared to be thoughtfully constructed and was surrounded by a circle of river rocks. The wood he'd used to build the fire must've been nice and dry. It had burned well, with almost nothing left in the ashes.

He also knew enough to put the fire out before he'd left—the ashes were wet. The commander must have doused them with the water from the river. Or maybe he'd just peed on them the way some of my male friends liked to do. The thought made me snicker, and I shook my head.

Nearby, I found the empty container from the leftover chili.

"Littering," I muttered under my breath, picking it up. "Not cool, Commander, not cool."

My alien now had no more food on him. Maybe hunger would slow him down enough for me to catch up with him?

Despite getting tired, I decided against taking a break. Grabbing a granola bar out of my backpack, I kept going.

Chapter 8

Commander

Annoying, meddlesome, cursed creatures!

The insects were everywhere. The buzzing cloud of them perpetually hung over his head, no matter how furiously he lashed his tails around, trying to chase them away. He lost count of their stings.

Every now and then, he'd drop his bundle of supplies to stop and scratch the bites thoroughly. But that only provided a temporary relief, forcing him to stop and scratch again a few paces later.

The little demons pierced through the flimsy material of his uniform. Unlike the clothes he wore into combat, the indoor uniform was designed to be lightweight and breathable. Its material provided little protection against the wilderness of this little-known planet.

Eventually, his entire body seemed to be one large bite side, driving him mad with itching. He took his uniform off and scratched until dark-red welts from his fingernails formed and filled with blood. Yet the relief was short-lived.

"Cursed little spawns of the Damned!" he bellowed into the woods, nearly driven to insanity by the incessant itching.

A snapping of a branch behind him made him whip around.

A large black animal stood under the trees. It watched him intently with its small round eyes. Clacking its long, pointed teeth, it lowered its head to the ground, turning its ears back.

"And what do you want?" he snapped at the creature. At least this one was big enough to punch, unlike the evasive bugs that had been torturing him for hours.

The animal pounded its great front paws on the ground while huffing, which appeared threatening.

"Well, bring it on!" he challenged, fisting his hands and spreading his tails, ready to lash.

The creature charged.

Lori

CAMPFIRE SMOKE FILTERED between the trees. I must be catching up to the commander. There simply was no one else around to start a fire.

It was about time, really. I'd been trudging through the woods most of the day, with one brief stop in the afternoon to catch my breath and rest my legs. It was getting dark already, and I was considering stopping for the night soon.

A little further up, I detected a distinct flavor in the smoke—the smell of roasted wild meat. My stomach growled. I still had plenty of granola bars left, a can of beans, and two cans of ravioli in my backpack, but I'd hardly had any time to eat, rushing to catch up with the commander all day.

The light of fire twinkled between the tree trunks in the distance. As if sensing the chance to finally get some rest, my feet sped up almost on their own.

The commander sat close to the fire, enveloped in the cloud of smoke. I blew out a breath of relief—he was alive.

"Lori?" He jumped to his feet as I approached. "What are you doing here?"

He sounded shocked, but I couldn't see his expression. Judging by the abundance of smoke from the fire, he must've used freshly chopped wood, not the dry weathered one this time.

Chunks of meat, spit on twigs, roasted over the flames. Placed on two flat rocks, water bubbled in the pot from my cabin. I hadn't even noticed the pot was gone when I left.

"How did you get here?" The commander seemed to have regained his composure, but I caught notes of concern and surprise in his voice.

"Well, I walked. Just like you." I shrugged the rifle off my shoulder. The freaking thing had been getting heavier with every step.

"It's not safe here," he said sternly. "You can get lost or attacked by animals."

Well, he knew the risks, at least.

"Listen. I've been walking in these woods since I was six. I know what I'm doing and where I am." I dropped my backpack down too, stretching my shoulders. "What I really need to know is where the hell do *you* think you're going?"

He stared at me grimly through the puffs of smoke.

"How did you find me?" he asked, not answering my question.

I scoffed. "That was the easy part. You move like a tank, leaving a wide trail for anyone to follow."

"You've had training," he stated, narrowing his eyes at me.

"Of course I have. Grandpa taught me since I was a kid."

"No. You work for the Coalition," he said in a grave voice.

"What coalition?"

It took me a moment to catch up that he was back to the same nonsense again.

"The Coalition of Earth's Governments. They sent you to apprehend me." He widened his stance.

Great, now he went from suspicions to accusations. I never knew I could be disliked in so many ways.

"Okay, so." I crossed my arms on my chest, spreading my feet wider, too. "I'm not sure what you've added to that smoke there, but I think you've been sitting way too close to it—you've lost your mind. You *know* I work for the Starlight Spacelines. I fly the shuttle. That's all I do."

"A perfect cover for a spy," he mumbled stubbornly.

"Hold on a minute. You really think I'm a spy?" The notion was too ridiculous to be angry about it. I laughed.

The commander didn't share my amusement. His severe expression hardened.

"Then, why are you here?" he interrogated.

I threw my hands up in the air.

"Because I had to make sure you didn't drown in the river or get eaten by a bear!"

"A bear?"

"Yes, a large, black animal with long teeth and claws. They rarely attack, but if they do, they can cause some serious damage to unsuspecting aliens who prance in the woods unattended."

"Like that animal?" He tipped his chin at the dark pile of fur that was barely visible in the distance behind the tree trunks. "If so, I'm about to eat *him*." He pointed at the meat roasting on the fire.

"You killed a bear?" I blinked at him, shocked and not a little impressed. "With just a hunting knife?"

He shook his head.

"I didn't bother taking the knife out."

"With your bare hands, then?" I opened my eyes wider. Judging by the black mass behind the trees, the beast was well above average in size.

The commander shrugged.

"He attacked me first."

"Black bears don't usually attack people," I muttered, flabbergasted. At least he didn't need a hunting permit if it was in self-defense.

"Well, nobody told *him* that," he retorted sarcastically. "To be fair, he might've tried to back off from the fight once he realized he was losing."

"But you didn't let him?"

"I was hungry." He bent over to turn the meat on the makeshift spit.

The wisps of smoke between us irritated my eyes, and I walked around them to see him better.

The commander's white uniform lay in a roll on the ground. He was wearing my navy-colored Snuggie, with the opening to the front. Straightening, he wrapped the ends of the blanket around his middle to cover up. I spotted long scratches on his face, arms, and head. Fresh smears of blood glistened on his night-colored skin.

"You're hurt!" I made a move toward him, but he stopped me by lifting a hand.

"I'm fine," he said firmly.

"Was it the bear? We need to treat the scratches as soon as possible before they get infected." I rushed to my backpack to get out my first-aid kit.

"I'll survive an infection." He reached inside the Snuggie to scratch his shoulder. "But these little demons from the fiery pits of Ahell will make me jump into the river, soon. Head first."

"Little demons?" I lifted my head, looking around. What was he talking about again? "Oh, you mean the mosquitos?" It dawned on me as he kept scratching, moving from his shoulder to his chest.

Mosquitos were in abundance this time of the year—or any time of the year, really, whenever the temperatures climbed above freezing.

"Yeah, mosquitoes are vicious around here," I said sympathetically, searching for the anti-itch cream in my first-aid kit.

"They don't seem to like the smoke very much," he said, clearly proud to have figured it out.

"Right. Bug spray works better, though."

"You have some with you?" he asked, his tone hopeful.

"I've got lots. I always carry it on me. But we need to treat the bites you've got, first." I eyed the hives and welts on his skin critically, assessing the damage. "Scratching only makes the itch worse, by the way."

"As if it's possible not to scratch," he grumbled.

"I know, right?" I felt genuinely sympathetic. Being bitten wasn't fun. I unscrewed the top of the tube with the anti-itching cream and handed it to him. "Here, put this on the hives. Try to avoid the scratches. It will sting if the skin is broken."

He took it from me and sniffed at it carefully.

I rolled my eyes at his suspiciousness, then heaved a sigh.

"I said I'm not trying to harm you, Commander. I'm not a spy." I stared him straight in the eye. "I've no idea where you came up with that nonsense or why you keep holding on to it, but I am who I say I am, Lori Soranno, a pilot for Starlight, and captain of a space shuttle. I may be your abductor, in this particular case, but I'm not a spy."

Abductor, kidnapper... Possibly a stalker, too, now. Tracking him in the woods could be viewed as stalker-ish, couldn't it?

I heaved a sigh. He had every right to be suspicious. At this point, I just wanted to get him back where I'd taken him from, in the best shape possible.

As he smeared the anti-itching cream on the welts and hives all over his arms and legs, worry flared in me anew. There was no way we would avoid questions when I got him back to the Conqueror. Surely, his crew would want to know where he'd been and how he'd ended up in this condition.

"I promised to take you back this morning," I said. "I would've delivered on my promise. You would've been in the city by now, had you not left in the middle of the night. Why did you go?"

He avoided looking at me, shifting his eyes toward the woods to the right, instead.

"I can't have you fly me back," he said after a pause.

"Why not?" His questioning of my skills and abilities earlier came to mind. Was he scared of flying with a woman? "I am a good pilot, you know. I've been flying since I was sixteen, with no accidents or violations. I have thousands of flight hours, on various equipment—"

He lifted his hand up, stopping me.

"Lori, I don't doubt your skills as a pilot."

"Not *anymore*, huh?" I tilted my head, squinting at him. "You did question them last night."

"I was impatient to return to my ship as soon as possible and wasn't thinking rationally enough," he said slowly, as if choosing his words carefully.

"Does it mean you're sorry?"

"About what?" His eyebrow ridges lifted.

"About questioning my skills as a pilot last night."

He stared at me for a long moment. His frown smoothed out somewhat.

"I'm sorry," he said finally.

"Good." I accepted his apology with a nod. "Now, why don't you want me to fly you back?"

His chest rose with another deep breath.

"I can't be seen with you."

His words stung. I sucked in a lungful of air that came with a hefty dose of smoke, which sent me into a coughing fit.

"Are you okay?" He stepped closer.

"Fine," I managed between the bouts of coughing. "Why not? Why can't you be seen with me?"

It might be best for my ego and my self-confidence not to know, but I didn't feel like I had much to lose at that point. The commander already thought me a spy and a kidnapper. What difference would it make if I learned he also thought me a butt-ugly monster not fit to be seen with in public?

He sat on the ground, resting his forearms on his bent knees.

"I can't tell you that," he said, casting me a glance from under his heavy brow.

Was he sparing my feelings? I bit my lip. The next moment, he frowned again, reaching back to scratch his shoulder blade.

"Do you have bites on your back, too?" I asked.

He roared a long string of words that my translator only conveyed as "fuck."

"I have them everywhere," he groaned.

I snatched the tube of cream from his hand and gestured at the Snuggie blanket. "Take it off."

"You want me to disrobe?" he asked, somewhat hesitantly.

I huffed in exasperation.

"I'm not trying to get naked in the woods with you, Commander. Trust me, sex is the furthest thing on my mind right now."

"It is?" He looked at me closely, his expression changing. His brow smoothed, and his mouth relaxed. His eyelids dropped a little, the thick black eyelashes shading his eyes. "I wish I could say the same," he muttered under his breath.

Oh God, what could he possibly mean by that? Surely, it had nothing to do with me—he hated my guts.

The way he stared at me, however, reminded me of the look he'd given me back on the Conqueror. A charge of heat rushed between us. Suddenly, I wished I could *disrobe* myself. My jeans felt too tight, my shirt stifling.

I fingered the top button of my shirt, swallowing hard.

"You don't have to...um, *disrobe*," I mumbled, nearly twisting the stupid button off. "You could just let it off your shoulders for me to put the cream on your back. Or you know what... Best try to do it yourself."

"No!" He quickly shrugged the blanket off his shoulders, turning his back to me. "Please, do it. I can't reach, and I can't stand the itching."

Angry reddish-black hives covered the entire expanse of his dark skin. Deep welts from his fingernails crisscrossed his back wherever he could reach.

I crouched down since he remained sitting on the ground.

"This looks brutal," I said softly, compassion tightening around my heart. "Does it hurt?" I hovered my fingers over his back, afraid my touch might cause him more pain.

"Not as much as it itches," he replied with a muffled groan.

I squeezed some cream from the tube on my finger, then started working from the top down his back, applying the cream on every bite bump while trying to avoid the scratches. His muscles rippled under my touch, and I couldn't help but notice there were a lot of muscles.

A shudder ran across his wide shoulders as I came to the small of his back. The blanket pooled here, covering him below the waist.

"Anywhere else?" I asked, after having treated everything I could see.

He muttered something under his breath, shifting uneasily.

I realized that the only untreated place that remained was his buttocks. I cleared my throat, glad my blush wouldn't be too apparent in the darkness thickening around us. The glow of the campfire would surely mask it, too.

"Well... I got most of it." I reached into my pocket for the cap to close the tube. There was no way he'd let me touch his naked butt.

"Wait." He stopped me. "There's more where I can't see."

He rose to his feet. Standing with his back to me, he dropped the Snuggie down, all the way past his knees.

I stared at his ass, muttering, "You want me to cream your bum."

Hard curves of his firm buttocks, slightly touched by the glow of the campfire, drew my attention like a magnet. His tails stretched down the middle. They stirred and twitched as he gave me a puzzled look over his shoulder.

"What did you just say?" he asked.

"Um... I was talking about putting this cream on your, um...behind," I hurriedly explained.

"That's not how my implant translated it." Amusement shone in his eyes.

I cringed inside, thinking about all the mortifying ways his translator could've put the words "cream" and "bum" into a sentence together.

My face grew so hot, I doubted even the glow of an erupting volcano would've masked my blush now.

"Linguistic differences…" I mumbled.

I'd thought it couldn't be any worse for the commander to think me an ugly stalker and a spy. Now, he could possibly add "a creep" to that list, too.

"Let's just…um…do this. Shall we?" I pointed with the tube of the cream at his ass.

"Go ahead." He gave me an easy smile.

The amusement never left his eyes, relaxing his usually hard expression. Deep dimples creased his cheeks on both sides as he smiled.

Dammit, the commander was a handsome man.

Biting my lip, I quickly got back to work. His tails trembled slightly, their ends concealed by the blanket pooled at his feet. Making sure I covered every visible bump and hive, I tried not to think about how firm his butt looked and felt. Yet my face kept burning hot. The heat shifted down my chest. It trickled all the way to my lower belly as I crouched down to get the hives on the back of his hard-muscled thighs, too.

Once that was finished, I also sprayed his back with the insect repellant to keep the mosquitoes away.

"All done." I released a breath, stepping back.

He didn't cover up or turn around, and I took a moment to admire his perfect form. The hard curves of his well-built body, covered in dark purple skin that was glistening in the dancing light of the fire, made him look like a fragment of the night itself.

"Thank you." He glanced over his shoulder at me.

Realizing he'd caught me ogling his ass, I blinked rapidly.

"That meat is probably burning hot and ready," I said quickly, trying to hide my gaze somewhere—anywhere—but it kept pivoting back to his naked form that towered in the woods like some kind of otherworldly forest spirit.

For someone who'd made a fuss about "disrobing" before, he sure seemed comfortable standing almost completely naked in front of me now.

"I'm not sure what you just said, Lori." A laugh bubbled in his voice. "But I'm certain it was not what the translator told me."

Mortified, I snapped my gaze to his. He met it with a teasing smile, his eyebrow ridge cocked. Was the commander simply amused or was he flirting with me? He still didn't pull up the blanket, letting me admire his butt to my heart's content.

What was it that I'd said?

"Meat? Hot and ready? Oh, God..." I groaned, scrubbing my hand over my face. "I was talking about *this* meat!" I gestured wildly at the pieces sizzling by the fire. "That translator of yours needs updating or something," I groaned.

"It's an older model," he admitted. Mercifully, he finally dragged the blanket up to cover his *assets*. "I should've upgraded it a while back but didn't find the time. I'm glad I didn't. It's making me laugh now." He chuckled.

I liked the sound of his laugh, even more than the sound of his voice. If it was at all possible.

The commander moved to the fire to take the meat off it.

"Dinner is ready." He took the pot of water off the rocks, too.

"Oh, I have some tea for that." Happy to focus on mundane things again, I rummaged in my backpack for a tin can with tea bags. I then tossed a couple in the pot.

He sliced up the meat on one of the rocks, searing the freshly cut sides, then offered me a piece on the tip of his knife.

"I've got salt, too." I took out two plastic shakers, handing one to him. "And lots of pepper for you."

"Pepper." A wide smile spread on his face at the sight of the shaker. "The best spice ever."

I gave him my Swiss Army knife so he could eat with me. Wild meat wasn't always the best tasting, but it turned out pretty good this time. After hiking almost the entire day, I was really hungry.

"So, will you tell me where you were going?" I asked, after swallowing a bite.

He glanced at me from under his brow but said nothing.

"Commander, I have no hidden agenda," I said with an exasperated sigh. "I came here all the way to help you. And you keep looking at me as if I were about to sell you to your worst enemies."

He remained quiet, obviously not trusting me one bit. I had only myself to blame for that. Regaining his trust wouldn't be easy.

"Commander, I'm truly sorry for taking you without your permission. Yesterday, the situation got out of control, but I want to rectify it now. If you have a plan, I'll help you accomplish it. But there is absolutely nothing in the direction you're heading. I'm afraid you're simply losing time."

"Nothing?" He shifted uneasily.

"Not a soul," I assured him confidently.

He seemed to consider my words for a moment.

"How about Rocky Point? According to your map, it's less than a day from here."

"Rocky Point?"

It would take longer than a day for someone like me to reach it. However, the commander certainly could cover the distance that quickly. If it wasn't for the mosquitoes slowing him down, I would've never caught up with him.

"Why Rocky Point?" I asked. "What's there? Is someone picking you up?"

He shook his head.

"It's the closest town, according to your map. From there, I intend to obtain transportation to the city."

That would work, had he not based his plan on severely outdated facts. The map was at least a decade old. I kept it mostly as a memento of my grandpa—by now, its value was more sentimental than practical. I still used it occasionally, but I was aware of discrepancies about which the commander couldn't know.

"There is nothing in Rocky Point," I told him. "No one lives there anymore. It's just a dot on the map."

His expression grew guarded again.

"What do you mean?"

"Years ago, Rocky Point was a hamlet, with three families living off the grid. The kids have all grown and left. The parents got older. Some passed away. Others moved to the city, closer to their children. There is nothing but three boarded up, dilapidating log cabins there."

His brow furrowed, making the piercings in the middle move closer together.

"Is that true? Or are you trying to make me change my course?"

I huffed a breath, rolling my eyes. I had no one to blame for his mistrust but myself and maybe Maddy's trigger-happy fingers. I'd apologized, however, and was ready to help him in any way he wished. Would he ever forgive me and move on?

"I'm trying to spare you days of useless trekking through the woods, Commander." I stared straight into his dark-violet eyes, willing him to believe me. "I'm being absolutely honest here. There is not one single reason for me to lie."

He worked his jaw, contemplating my words.

"What is the closest town, then?" he asked.

"Mirror Lake. It's pretty big. It even has a grocery store."

"How far is it from here?"

"On foot? It'd probably take you three-four days. But I can fly you there—"

"No." He shook his head resolutely. "Your aircraft is registered in your name, is it not?"

So, not only did he not want to be seen with me, he didn't even want my airplane anywhere near him?

"There is no airport in Mirror Lake," I said flatly. "I'd be landing in an open field. No one will see you with me—if that's what you're afraid of."

"I'm not afraid," he scoffed. "An Ivodian is never afraid of anything."

"If you say so." I didn't hide sarcasm, getting up and brushing dead pine needles off my jeans.

He would fight a bear with his bare hands, but the slightest possibility of being seen with me terrified him enough to send him hiking through the woods for days.

Chapter 9

Lori

I got the shelter roll out of my backpack.

"How were you planning to spend the night, Commander?"

He poured the water he'd brought from the river over the smoldering coals in the fireside. He wasn't like my male friends after all. He didn't pee on the fire to put it out, at least not in my presence.

"Climb the tree, tie myself to the trunk," he replied to my question.

The commander obviously wasn't a stranger to surviving in the wild.

"That's a pretty good plan." I nodded with approval. "If a cougar doesn't find you, that is."

"What's a cougar?" He picked up his uniform from the ground and shook the old leaves and pine needles out of it.

After I'd sprayed him and the Snuggie with the bug spray, the commander finally stopped itching.

"A large cat," I explained, unfurling the tent. "They climb trees."

"I'm not afraid of cats," he scoffed.

"Of course." I smiled. "You're not afraid of cougars, and you fight bears naked. It's the mosquitos that get you."

He winced, his hand going to a dark hive on the side of his neck.

I swatted his hand away.

"No itching, remember?"

"Little, blood-sucking, foul creatures," he muttered under his breath, but took his hand away without touching the bite side.

"Well," I patted his hand reassuringly. "For someone completely new to this area—and to Earth in general—you did amazingly well,

76

Commander. Honestly, I feared I'd find you cold, lost, and hungry, or maybe even no longer alive."

He leveled me a stare then raised his chin proudly.

"I have endured much harsher climates than this one and survived far more perilous situations."

"You did? How?" I was surprised and genuinely curious. "I thought the Ivodians mostly stayed on the ship and shot their weapons."

"We conquer, but we also explore. I've trekked many planets. Lori."

The sound of my name stroked my arms with a shiver of tingles, like it always did whenever he said it. I could listen to his voice forever.

I stifled a sigh.

"You must have some cool stories to tell," I said wistfully.

I'd become a space shuttle pilot, hoping to travel to other worlds one day, but I had yet to make it even past the Earth's orbit.

"I do," he said. "I have plenty of stories. Telling them would take many campfire nights."

Suddenly, I wished we had many nights ahead of us, to spend them just like this, camping together and talking by the fire. What wouldn't I give to hear his stories.

I shook my head, trying to get rid of the empty dreams.

"Well, it's time to go to bed," I said, opening the entrance flap of the shelter. "I only brought one tent. It's big enough for three people, and you're welcome to share it with me."

The commander went quiet. I glanced over my shoulder at him. He either was considering my offer or went silent in shock, probably appalled by my proposition.

He'd been so cautious and guarded around me, I felt compelled to clarify. "You know I don't mean anything by it. Promise, I'll keep my clothes on and my hands off you," I added with a smile, in an attempt to lighten the tension hanging between us.

He didn't return my smile.

"Sharing a sleeping space would be a big mistake," he finally said.

A big mistake.

My entire existence in his life was nothing but a huge mistake, wasn't it? I bit my lip and turned away, trying to hide the sting of bitterness his words had caused.

"Well, good night then," I mumbled, crawling into the tent on my own.

Shortly after I settled into my sleeping bag, however, I heard the zipper of the tent open again.

"I didn't mean to upset you." The commander crawled in. Fully dressed in his uniform, he was dragging his Snuggie behind him.

"I'm not upset." I rolled over to the wall of the tent, away from him.

"Yes, you are. If there's anything I've learned about human women, it's how to tell when they're upset. Not all of them were thrilled to be on the Conqueror, and many didn't hesitate to let us know."

I lay still, saying nothing.

"I know you're upset, but I'm not sure about your reasons for feeling this way," he added, stretching behind me.

Was he really that clueless? He was an alien, not an emotionless robot or an unfeeling machine. Did he not realize how his mistrust and suspicions affected me?

"Reasons?" I turned around to face him. "Fine. I'll tell you my reasons, Commander. You've been treating me like a plague or an enemy. I know I made a mistake by bringing you here. I've apologized for that, and I'm willing to do anything to fix it, but you're not giving me a chance to do it. You'd rather run through the woods, fight bears, and dodge cougars than risk being seen with me. Why is that? Do you think I'm too ugly? Too insignificant? Too low rank to be spotted in the company of the mighty commander?" My voice rang high with indignation I could no longer hide. "Are those not enough reasons for me to be upset?"

I drew in a shaky breath, fighting for composure.

"Yes, you have every right to dislike me," I continued. "But please give me a chance to make it better. Let me fix it. Don't make it worse."

My lower lip trembled, and I bit it again, struggling not to break down in front of him.

"Lori," he said softly, shifting closer. "I don't dislike you. I couldn't, even if I wanted to. Believe me, I tried. On the contrary..." He reached out to touch the side of my face, and I let him, subdued by the unexpected warmth in his voice. "My biggest problem right now is that I *like* you, much more than I should."

He sure had a weird way of showing it.

"I admire you," he continued. "I've never met a woman like you in my life, and I find you fascinating."

His confession sounded genuine. It rendered me speechless.

"Why is that a problem?" I asked tentatively when I finally found my voice again.

He drew in a breath, the curve of his mouth shifting into a firm line.

"No one can know you've abducted me. You promised not to tell anyone."

"And I won't, but I'd love to understand why it's so important for you. Even if the incident is reported, Maddy and I would be the ones facing disciplinary action. There shouldn't be any consequences for you. You're the victim here."

"Exactly. A fucking victim." He winced as if having bitten into something sour. "If anyone sees me with you, on your plane or anywhere near your property, they may connect my disappearance from the ship with you. If my warriors find out you took me, they will view it as an abduction."

"Why would it be an issue for them, though? Don't Ivodians take abduction as a perfectly acceptable thing? I haven't done anything to you that your warriors haven't done to our women. I didn't even chain you to my bed, which I've heard happened to some of our women on the Conqueror."

For a minute, he just lay there, breathing heavily.

"Men abduct women," he finally said, his expression grave. "Not the other way around."

"I don't see the difference." I shook my head, confused. "Don't Ivodians have equal rights for men and women?"

The limitations of Ivodian women came from their health conditions; they were not imposed on them by dominating men.

"The rights are equal," he agreed. "But the expectations of how the two genders are supposed to act are vastly different."

"I don't understand..."

He flopped on his back, staring up at the roof of the tent. The subject appeared difficult to discuss for him, but he continued, not meeting my eye. "For a woman to be taken by a warrior who has risked his life to earn the right to marry her, the abduction is an honor. For a man to be taken by a woman..." He heaved a sigh, shaking his head. "Well, I've never even heard of such a thing before."

"There's a first time for everything, isn't there?" I tried to lighten his mood. His desolate expression was breaking my heart.

He turned to me, propping himself on an elbow.

"If word came out that a woman outwitted and overpowered me, I'd lose the respect of my men."

"What?" I drew back from him. "How?"

"The commander has absolute power on the ship unless his crew deem him unfit to lead. If my warriors voted to remove me from my position, I'd lose everything I've worked for my entire life."

His words hit me like a punch in the gut.

"No..." I rose on my arm.

"Disgraced, I'd never be allowed to hold a position of leadership again," he continued in a hard, determined voice. "I would be demoted to the lowest rank, stripped of all privileges, including an honorable retirement and marriage. I'd be starting all over again, from the very bottom."

The longer he spoke, the bigger the dark blob of horror grew in my chest.

"I... I didn't know..." I whispered, sitting up. Tears prickled the insides of my eyelids. "I'm so, so sorry."

"And worst of all," he continued mercilessly, "I'd be forever known as the only man in history who was abducted by a woman. My family name would be stained for generations."

I covered my mouth with my hands, tears seeping through my shut eyelids. "I had no idea."

"I know." His warm hand cupped the side of my face. His thumb brushed a tear away. "I'm not angry with you, Lori, but I need to find a way to salvage the situation, if not for myself, then for the sake of my family, at least."

Opening my eyes, I stifled a sob, not trusting myself to speak.

"One way or another, I will get back to the Conqueror," the commander continued. "There will be an investigation when I come back, and I need to make sure there's no trace of evidence that would connect me to you. Do you understand?"

I sniffled, nodding. He really had been running away from me like from a plague. Only now I knew the reasons why.

"I fucked up. So badly," I whispered.

He touched my shoulder.

"From what I remember, it wasn't entirely your fault. The first officer was the one with the taser."

I shook my head.

"I'm the captain. Everything that happens at work is my fault and my responsibility."

He leaned closer.

"*That* I understand—the responsibility of a leader." He wrapped his arm around my shoulders and gently eased me back into the sleeping bag. "I blame myself for what happened, Lori, no one else. I'd been curious about you and jumped way too eagerly on the opportunity to talk to you face-to-face, forgetting all the caution."

"You were going to detain me," I reminded him.

He narrowed his eyes at me with a crooked smile, which bared a canine on one side. It gave him a rather predatory expression.

"I wanted to keep you," he admitted, drawing me closer. His tails slid over the sleeping bag, taking me into a whole-body hug. "I don't find you ugly or insignificant, Lori. I'd be honored to be seen in public with you..." His chest rose with a deep breath. "Under different circumstances."

"I'm so sorry I approached you at all, then..." I said between shuddered breaths.

"I'm not," he said unexpectedly. "I'm not sorry about that."

I stared at him through the blurry film of tears. "If I didn't leave the shuttle, none of this would've happened."

"Exactly." He swept a strand of my hair behind my ear. "From the moment I met you, you haven't stopped amazing me. Every minute with you has been a thrilling surprise. And I don't regret any of it."

He stroked my shoulder through my shirt. The light, rhythmic movement soothed me, luring me to close my eyes and relax. After the long hike, my body was begging for sleep. Snuggling against him, I felt warm and cozy.

I wasn't sure if it was real or if I dreamed it when the commander kissed my tear-stained face, whispering, "Happy Birthday, Lori. May you have a long life ahead of you and may these be the last tears you cry."

Chapter 10

Lori

The next morning, I woke alone in the tent.

"Commander?" I called, scrambling to the exit.

The thought that he might've gone ahead with his plan to hike to Mirror Lake speared through me with a shot of panic. The last words I'd heard him say before falling asleep, *"May you have a long life ahead of you and may these be the last tears you cry,"* sounded very much like a farewell.

Yanking the zipper of the tent flap open, I poked my head out. Relief flooded me when I saw the commander by the firepit arranging dry twigs in the shape of a tepee to start a fire. A much larger pile of dry wood lay nearby.

He lifted his head, smiling at me.

"Greetings," he said.

His expression was too friendly, considering I might've ruined his life. Guilt flooded me anew.

"Morning." I climbed out, rubbing my upper arms against the early hour chill. "I was afraid you were gone."

"The thought had crossed my mind," he confessed, using a lighter to start the fire.

"Why didn't you?"

"I couldn't possibly leave a woman alone in the middle of wild territory," he replied.

I couldn't hold back a snort.

"Commander, I grew up in these woods. Trust me, I know my way around."

"I believe you do. But it's a duty of every Ivodian man to ensure the safety of a woman. I'll walk you back to your shelter where you have plenty of food and water, as well as transportation. Then, I'll be on my way."

I opened my mouth to argue, then closed it. Of course, I could easily find my way back to the cabin. I had a rifle to defend myself if needed. Letting the commander escort me, however, provided the opportunity to talk him out of the long, perilous hike he'd planned. It would take us at least a day to get back to the cabin, longer if we stopped to rest. Maybe we could eventually come up with a better solution, together?

"Fine," I conceded. "I accept your services as my bodyguard for the next day or two."

To my surprise, he got up and gave me a formal bow.

"It will be my honor to guard you."

I didn't think the task required this level of formality. Clearing my throat, I gave him a quick nod.

"We'll have breakfast then fry some more meat for the road." The commander took charge, obviously taking his new job very seriously.

"I have a can of beans and some ravioli on me. A couple of granola bars are left, too."

"Is all of that food?" he asked.

"Yes. Non-perishables."

"We'll save them for when we run out of meat, then," he concluded.

He fried several long strips of meat and boiled some water over the fire. I folded the tent back up, then made some tea.

"It's pretty here." I sat on a log by the fire, a cup of tea in my hands.

My eyes half-closed, I inhaled the familiar, pine-rich scent of the woods, enjoying the quiet morning.

"It reminds me of the foothills in the mountains of Us'ae, a moon of Rimall," the commander said. "The color of the foliage is different. The forests on Us'ae are mostly deep blue and light brown, but the scent is very similar. So is the sense of tranquility."

I looked at him over the rim of my cup.

"You feel it, too?" I asked. "The serenity?"

Peace and quiet of this area were some of the reasons I never sold the cabin after grandpa died. Instead, I came here every chance I got. The woods were my happy place.

He nodded. "The breathing is easier here. Your mind grows...bigger."

"Bigger?" I tilted my head.

"Back on the Conqueror," he explained, "I have too many things to worry about, every minute of every day. When I go to Us'ae, I can think beyond the day-to-day activities. It's like my mind expands, encompassing more than I ever thought was possible."

That was exactly how I felt here. All mundane little things fell away, letting me...breathe freely and feel more deeply. Here, I was able to think about things bigger than my everyday life.

"Humans are very lucky to have places like this on Earth," the commander said.

"There aren't any on Ivodi?"

"No. Every habitable piece of land on my planet has been populated for centuries. That's how the warships came to be. Long ago, Ivodians fought to invade populated planets. Eventually, we started focusing on exploring the unpopulated ones, too." He started packing the leftover meat. "It's easier. No conflicts with the locals, more payoffs in terms of resources. We claim everything we find."

"Including women?" I couldn't help myself. "If the planet is populated, of course."

He looked at me straight on.

"Including women."

I blinked under his stare. He wasn't kidding. Silent, I packed the rest of our things.

The commander put out the fire by dumping a potful of river water on it, then took both his Snuggie bundle and my backpack. As I was about to sling the rifle over my shoulder, he took it from me, too.

"Hey," I protested. "Shouldn't I be carrying at least something?"

"No." He started on his way, taking off in long strides. "Just try to keep up."

Now that he'd been sprayed against the mosquitos, nothing was slowing him down.

"Keep up?" I hurried after him, adding defensively, "Why do you think I'll have any trouble keeping up with you?"

"I don't think you will." He flashed me a white-toothed grin.

I almost tripped over a tree root, seeing him smile at me like that, as if we were friends—no, more than friends if that flirty teasing spark in his eyes was anything to go by.

Regaining my balance, I matched my pace with his. After a while, I suspected he'd slowed down a bit to allow me to keep up more easily. I decided not to confront him about that because, well, the man could move way too fast for me. Even with the two packs and the heavy rifle, his long legs ate up the forest floor at a speed I'd never seen before.

Instead, I felt grateful for an easier pace that also allowed us to have a conversation.

"Do men train hard on the Ivodian warships?" I asked, panting slightly. They must, judging by the commander's great physical shape.

"Yes," he replied. "We go through years of intense training even before we join a ship."

"How many years?"

"I started school when I was five."

"Five? That young?" I exclaimed.

He shot me another grin. The commander seemed to be in a much better mood this morning. It must be the calming effect of the woods he'd spoken about.

"We start early because there's a lot to learn," he said.

"But how can you even be sure at that age what you'll want to be when you grow up?"

He shrugged. "For as long as I remember I've wanted to be a warrior, like my father. Serving on the warships is also one of the very few ways to earn the right to marry. It ensures a strong parental line, which is good for the future of our population."

The commander moved a leafy branch out of my way.

"Did your father work on the ships, too?"

"Yes, but he's long retired. My parents live on Ivodi."

I took a moment before asking the next question.

"Did, um, your dad abduct your mom?"

He nodded without hesitation.

"Of course he did. But their families knew each other. Their union was planned and arranged in advance. My father retired when he was thirty-eight, as an honorable commander of a warship. He then abducted my mother. They got married and had me."

"He retired early. Or is that a normal age for Ivodians?"

He held my elbow, helping me climb over a fallen log on our path.

"Most Ivodian warriors retire around their mid to late thirties. By that age, they have usually proven themselves at work and in battle and earned the right to have a wife. For their service, they're awarded the right to choose a piece of land on any of the pre-approved planets. They abduct a wife and start a family. When the children are grown and independent, the parents often resume their careers."

"They would go back to the ship?"

"No. Only the young and unmated men travel the space. There're plenty of jobs for the older people on Ivodi or wherever they choose to live. My father has been serving as an Advisor on the Central Council of all warships for over a decade now. My mother is one of the ten Elders of the Higher Chamber of the Ivodian Government."

"Wow, that sounds important," I gasped, impressed.

"She is a highly esteemed politician," he agreed.

"I thought you said your women stayed at home. That they're too fragile. Yet your mom works?"

"Many do. Our women are physically vulnerable, yes, but they're not feeble-minded. They're very capable. Many hold important positions in all spheres and every industry. My mother doesn't need to leave home to go to work. She attends all government sessions remotely, as a hologram. It's safer for her health."

His expression softened when he spoke about his mom and dad.

"Do you see your parents often?"

"As a hologram, once a week." His smile grew wider. "My mother insists on checking on me at least that often. In person, it's been ten years now since I've hugged them last." A note of wistfulness slipped into his voice.

Seeing him like that was new. The mighty commander was someone's son, who loved his parents.

"It helps to talk to them regularly, doesn't it?" I said. "My parents moved to Vancouver Island when they retired. It's all the way across the country. I don't get to see them very often, but I try to call them at least weekly. Just like you."

He cast me a curious glance.

"How did *your* parents get married?"

"Oh, they eloped." I smiled.

"Eloped?"

"Yes. They went to Jamaica—an island in the Caribbean Sea, south of here—without telling anyone. They got married there, then came back as a husband and wife."

"That sounds a lot like an abduction," he said thoughtfully.

"No, it isn't." I shook my head. "They planned to get married and went away together. No one snatched anyone."

"Is that how it's usually done on Earth?"

If the Ivodians researched anything about Earth before coming here, it was obvious their research on our marriage customs was lacking. At least he was asking about that now.

"There are lots of different cultures and marriage traditions on Earth," I explained. "But marriage here is normally a culmination of a relationship, not its beginning. When two people get married, they usually know each other well and have spent some time together."

"How?" He seemed genuinely interested to know.

"They date before getting married. Which means they live separately, but they make time to spend together."

"Why?"

Things we took for granted were a novelty to him. I scratched my nose, thinking of a way to explain.

"Because they like each other."

"Why do they live separately then if they like each other?"

The man was full of questions. He genuinely seemed to want to understand human marriages and relationships. Maybe he was still hoping to salvage whatever was left of their abduction spree? If so, he might be on the right path here. From what I'd seen, some of the women the Ivodians had returned might be open to reconciliation.

"Because just liking each other is not enough," I replied. "Some couples decide they don't want to be together after all."

"Why?"

I drew in a long breath.

"Well, they get to know each other better and realize they don't like the other person that much after all. Doesn't it happen for Ivodians, too? If a man snatches a woman in your world, doesn't she ever get upset about that?"

He shook his head.

"I've never heard about women being sad about being chosen by men, not until Earth."

"Really? They just go along with everything?"

"Abductions have been a part of Ivodian culture since the beginning of time. Women have always been scarce. Men fought for a chance to acquire a wife and reproduce. Only the best ones won the right to get married and perpetuate their line. Historically, all women would be claimed. If for any reason one went unclaimed, it was considered a great shame for her entire family. Ivodian girls were raised dreaming to be taken by a brave, mighty warrior one day."

I glanced at him suspiciously.

"You're speaking in the past tense. Is it no longer the way on Ivodi?"

He held another low-hanging branch out of the way for me and waited for me to pass.

"Abducting a bride is still the only way to get married on Ivodi," he said, easily catching up with me. "In modern times, however, politics, economics, and family connections play a much bigger role in forming a union. The groom is selected based on his achievements, and the bride often knows in advance who her abductor will be."

"Well, that's different from how you did it on Earth then, isn't it?"

"Not really," he objected. "Brides are always happy to be chosen and abducted. Women should be delighted to be claimed by Ivodian warriors."

"Delighted, huh?" I asked skeptically.

Was it even possible to explain anything to someone with such an unshakable self-confidence?

"Marrying an Ivodian warrior is a great honor," the commander continued. "As the wife of an Ivodian, a human woman will never want for anything. She'll live a happy, pampered life with the husband who will make it his mission to take care of her every need and want."

"Sounds lovely, but I do have a problem with the way you go about obtaining the wives. Since you've been returning all of them now, it appears they had a problem with that too, doesn't it?"

He inhaled deeply, his brow furrowing.

"I've never heard of a resistance this intense," he admitted. "I didn't expect human women to be this upset about being abducted."

"Really? You didn't?" I gave him a sideway glance, not hiding my sarcasm. "Do you remember how upset *you* were when you found yourself at my place?"

He winced. "That's different."

"How? Although it was not my intention, I did end up abducting you." I might as well admit it.

The muscles in his jaw flexed, and his eyes narrowed.

"You promised not to talk about it."

"With other people, no, I won't," I assured him. "But you and I should discuss it, don't you think? Who knows, it may even help you understand your failure at wooing our women."

"It's not a failure," he growled stubbornly. "Ivodian warriors don't fail."

"Yeah, okay." I propped my hands on my hips. "You came here to get some women, and you're leaving without them soon. That's not exactly what I'd call a success."

He tightened his grip on the straps of the rifle and the backpack. His knuckles protruded, and his tails lashed against the trunks of the trees we were passing by. A growl vibrated in his chest.

It didn't intimidate me, however.

"Growl all you want. Human women obviously weren't happy with your courting manners," I pointed out.

He huffed, clearly irritated.

"They would've come around. Good things don't take long to get used to. The women just needed more time to adjust to their new situations."

"I don't think so," I said resolutely. "You snatched them, taking them away from their homes and their loved ones, without their consent. There's no coming back from that."

He gave me a guarded glance.

"No?" he asked carefully.

"Nope." I firmly shook my head. "You see, most human women don't sit around waiting to be abducted. They aren't sheltered. They meet people every day, men and women. Some of those you've abducted already had men in their lives."

I knew for a fact that Felicity Davis did. There could've been others with boyfriends and fiancés.

"We don't abduct married women," he protested.

"Yeah, but the commitment for us often happens before marriage. Like I said, people usually start dating before getting married or moving in together."

We walked in silence for a little while. The commander appeared to be mulling my words, and I let him to it.

"Do human women find Ivodians attractive?" he asked unexpectedly, catching me off guard.

"Um... Sure." I blinked, avoiding his eyes and praying my face wouldn't turn flaming red again.

Thankfully, the commander appeared to be deep in thought.

"So, physical attraction is not the problem, then?" he asked, his expression contemplative.

Definitely not on my part.

I cleared my throat, forcing myself to think in general terms.

"Physical attraction? You mean the looks? No, that is not a problem... I mean, I can't speak for every woman out there but, generally, I think your crew are very handsome. But keep in mind, appearance is not everything. Some of the women you took already were committed to a human man. Some just never would fall for you, no matter what you do. Keep in mind, some human women prefer other women to any men, human or alien, no matter how attractive men may be."

"They do?" He cocked his head. "Well, that makes it even more complicated, doesn't it?"

"It does," I agreed.

"So, how would you go about this, were you in our place?" he suddenly asked.

I held my breath, not a little shocked. Was the commander of the Conqueror asking my advice? He seemed rather humble about it, too.

"Well," I started slowly, carefully choosing my words. "First of all, I would study human culture long before coming here. That would be hundreds of cultures, actually, because Earth's population is not homogenous. It comprises a multitude of countries and groups within the countries. The main thing, though, is that women need to have a say in this whole thing. You have to give them a choice."

"Do you mean let the women choose their mates?" He arched an eyebrow ridge, staring at me incredulously. "That would never work for Ivodians. A man abducts his woman, not the other way around."

I blew out a frustrated breath. "Why does anyone have to abduct someone, at all?"

"Because it's tradition," he insisted stubbornly.

"Traditions change, don't they?"

"Not this one," he protested. "Not overnight. Not on one single ship out of thousands. The warriors will never agree to anything like that because if they did, they know they wouldn't be able to show their faces back on Ivodi ever again. They'd be disgraced."

"Okay, okay I get it." I lifted my hands in a pacifying gesture. "For Ivodians, it's great to abduct women, but it's absolutely the worst to abduct men. How about letting women *choose* their abductor, then? You said some marriage arrangements happen on Ivodi, before the actual abduction takes place, right? How about letting your men and our women mingle beforehand, too? Give a woman a chance to figure out which one of your warriors she likes, then send that one to get her."

He worked his jaw, sharp focus in his eyes.

"What if more than one man will want the same woman?"

"Well, there's always that risk, but we're all adults, we can sort out those things peacefully—"

"No," he cut me off resolutely. "A warrior will fight to the death for his chosen one. If I allow my men to mingle with unclaimed women, fights will happen. I'll lose men."

"Great," I muttered under my breath. "I was kinda hoping you guys were capable of resolving conflicts in a civilized manner, not by killing each other."

He shrugged. "Once a warrior has chosen a woman, she's his. Taking her from him is an offense, punishable by death."

"Is it? Really?" I thought back to all my shuttling the abducted women back to Earth. "How did you even manage to make them give up their bounty, then? It must've been hard."

He heaved a breath.

"You have no idea. I've used my authority to the limit on that one. My crew was ready to declare a war on the Coalition and the entire Earth."

"Why did you do it, then? Why did you agree to return the women?" I knew the commander well enough by now to understand the decision was not a simple change of heart on his part. He didn't suddenly turn sympathetic and let the women go.

"I had my reasons," he said evasively.

Sadly, he still didn't trust me completely.

"Okay, fine." I let it go for now, no matter how much I wished to know his reasons. "How about making the selection process private, then? You can create a database of all your eligible warriors. Post a picture of each, make them write something about themselves."

"Like what?" He seemed intrigued. "You mean their achievements, most successful missions, and the number of kills?"

Oh boy, it wasn't easy with him.

"Actually, I was thinking about things like their favorite food and what they like doing for fun. But sure, missions and achievements could also be included, why not?" I waved a hand, giving up. "Let's just skip the number of kills for now, okay?"

He nodded, looking focused. Hopefully, he was paying attention and taking mental notes.

"Then," I continued, developing my plan as I went, "You'll make the database public, so all interested women on Earth can see it. They would be able to express their interest in the profiles of the warriors whom they'd like to get to know better. Each woman would be allowed to select just one man at a time. Then, the warriors would choose which one of the women on their profiles they would like to take out on a date."

"A date? Which is spending time together, you said."

"Right. You remember." I smiled, happy he'd paid attention. "The Ivodian warriors then can travel to Earth to take the women out for dinner or invite them to the Conqueror to watch a movie or something. Do you have movies? It's like a make-believe story played out by actors on a screen?"

"We do." He nodded. "But will watching a movie with a man make a woman agree to the abduction by him?" He sounded skeptical.

"It's not the movie, it's the man and his behavior during the date that will help her decide. That's when they get to know each other. The important part is that she should be able to say no, at any time. Do you understand? There is always a risk she would say no. Then she should be let go. But if she says yes, every step of the way, then she'd likely be happy to get abducted, too. She'd be more willing to commit, and her commitment would be stronger than any chains you guys use to tie women to your beds."

"Chains?" he asked, looking puzzled.

"I've heard that's what you do. You tie women to your beds." He kept staring at me, and I exhaled a laugh, somewhat nervously. "No? Must be just a silly rumor, then."

Something in his gaze wouldn't let me relax, however. His eyes half-hooded by his eyelids, he slid his gaze down my body as if measuring it for size.

"Not a rumor," he said with a low rumble in his voice that made it sound soft and luxurious, like velvet. His top lip curved in a smile that bared his canines, giving him a predatory appearance once again. "Except that we don't use *chains*."

His tails rose from behind him. Sleek and graceful, they arched around his shoulders, reaching for me.

My breath hitched.

"How about *you*, Lori?" he murmured. "Do *you* find Ivodian men attractive?"

Curved like tight strung bows, his tails trembled as if ready to snap. Each tip aimed at a certain point on my body, from my head to my toes.

What would happen if he unleashed them on me? Anticipation pulsed inside me. I had no idea what Ivodians did with their tails, but I would love to find out.

The commander looked like he was ready to show me, but he wouldn't move any further.

Of course he wouldn't. He'd said he needed to get *away* from me, not get closer. Some things would make the getting-away part harder, I feared, for him as much as for me. It was best not to let them happen.

I took a few deep breaths, counting my heartbeats until the butterflies in my stomach settled down somewhat.

"Of course I do, Commander. I find Ivodian men very attractive." I plastered a big smile on my flushed face. "I even tried to snatch one for my own, remember?"

The reminder of our situation was enough to cool both of us off. The smoldering hot expression slipped off his face. The tails moved away to trail quietly behind him again. My heart pinched with disappointment at the thought that I would never find out what they felt like when slinking along my body.

I dropped my gaze down, not sure how to deal with the charged silence that descended on us like a soft fuzzy cloud. Even the steady noise of the water rushing over the rocks of the river nearby fell away.

"You make me question the order of things," the commander said softly. "Shaking my respect for rules and traditions."

I raised my eyes to his.

"I never meant to be disrespectful…" My voice came out as almost a whisper. I struggled not to get lost in the violet midnight of his eyes.

"It's not about your intentions or your actions, Lori. It's your mere existence that makes me wish things were different."

Chapter 11

Lori

"Let's get closer to the river over there, Commander." I pointed at the path between two fallen trees, recognizing the place. "I'll show you one of my most favorite spots out here."

It was a little too early to stop for lunch, but we'd made good progress so far. A short break wouldn't slow us down too much.

The commander followed me along the path. Parting the underbrush, I stepped out on the rocky riverbank. A wide creek merged with the river on the opposite side, which was higher than the one we stood on. The water from the creek bubbled and rolled between the rocks in a cascading waterfall.

"This is beautiful," the commander said as we admired the bubbling waterfall, framed by light-green underbrush and the majestic dark pine trees of the forest.

"I knew you'd like it." I smiled, feeling exceptionally pleased about that. We hadn't spent much time together, but I'd learned quite a bit about the commander's likes and dislikes already. The fact that we seemed to like similar things warmed my heart with added pleasure. "Not many people have seen it. I think that gives this place a special charm, the remoteness of it. Every time I come here, I feel like I've landed in another world."

We sat on the rocks, listening to the soothing sound of rushing water.

"Let's have lunch here," the commander suggested.

"Are you hungry?"

"I could eat." He grinned. "I always could eat."

There was no need to build a fire. We ate what was left of the fried meat with a side of beans from the can.

"What are these things?" the commander had asked skeptically when I'd opened the can.

"Fried beans with pork. It's kind of like chili," I explained, shifting the can closer to him to give him a better look.

He sniffed the contents of the can, then took some with the spoon of my Swiss Army knife. He curved his mouth in distaste after the first bite.

"This is nothing like your chili," he scoffed.

"You're quite a picky eater, aren't you?" I poked him in his side with my elbow.

He chuckled, shoving another spoonful of beans in his mouth.

"Oh, I'm not picky. I'll eat anything when I'm on a mission," he said after chewing and swallowing. "But I always appreciate a tasty meal. Your chili is incomparable to anything I've ever had. I had to have the leftovers, too, even as I was leaving your dwelling."

I laughed, pleasure spreading warm through my chest at his praise. I was sure my face radiated the glow, too.

"Thank you. That's the best compliment a cook could have. I'll make it for you—" I cut myself short. I wanted to say I'd cook it for him any time he wished, but there never would be another time. This was it. These hours in the woods were all we had. My mood plummeted, and I mumbled, "I mean I'm glad you liked it."

He must've sensed the change in me. His lavender eyes stared at me intently. Flustered under his gaze, I crouched by the water to rinse the empty can and the utensils, then packed them away.

"Well, we should keep going." I said after he finished his food, too, and we both had some water to wash it down.

The commander remained seated, however. "I don't want to."

"You don't want to go?" I asked, confused.

He shook his head, staring at the river.

"Not yet. When do you have to be back in the city, Lori?"

"Monday night. I work Tuesday. My flight is early in the morning." He turned to me.

"Today is Sunday, according to your calendar, with Monday and Tuesday next, right?"

I nodded.

"We've covered a good distance already. Even if we stay here for the night, we'll still be at your cabin early afternoon tomorrow. You'll make it to the city early enough to have a good sleep on Monday before going to work on Tuesday."

"You want to stay here overnight?" My heart gave a loud thud. He was right. There was no reason for me to rush to the city before Tuesday. The more time I spent with the commander, the more I could learn about the Ivodian way of life, the stronger was the chance for me to figure out what to do.

If his main goal was to get away from me as far as possible so that the rest of his warriors never suspected any connection between his disappearance and me, then maybe I could still convince him to accept a ride from me. I would fly him half the way across the world if it meant sparing him the risk and trouble of hiking through the woods for days.

He tilted his head, keeping his intense stare on me.

"It's a beautiful place. I want more time to enjoy it," he said slowly.

I couldn't deny him that.

"We'll stay." I smiled with a brief nod.

We set up the tent right by the rocks on the riverbank, with the view of the waterfalls. The commander started the fire, and I boiled some water for tea.

After taking all the contents out of his makeshift bundle, the commander shook out the Snuggie.

"This is one of the most practical garments I've ever seen." He threaded his arms in the sleeves, wearing it backwards like a cape.

"Is it?" I hid a giggle behind my hand. "It's not exactly for camping, you know."

"Why not?" He looked genuinely surprised. "It's perfect for camping. You can wear it through the day then sleep under it at night."

He did have a point. Being significantly taller than me, the blanket didn't trail on the ground behind him that much. His tails lifted the hem slightly, keeping it above the forest floor. Grabbing one side of it, he threw it over his shoulder with a majestic gesture that brought a Roman Emperor to mind.

"It was designed literally to sit on the couch and watch TV." I laughed. "But you do make it look so much more than that. I guess they're right, clothes don't make the man."

He sat on the fallen log by the fire with me.

"I wish I had this garment on when I climbed the mountain of Varae."

"Are you into mountain climbing?" I asked, curious. I'd never done that myself, but I admired the endurance and agility of those who did it regularly. "Was it during a holiday?"

He rested a forearm on his knee.

"No. I was on a mission for Ivodi. I needed to get a frozen lava sample from the crater of Varae for the Counsel. The shuttle dropped me off as close as it could get without being shot down by the hostile locals. I had to climb along icy crevices, carrying as few supplies on me as possible."

His life sounded more and more like a movie to me, full of risk and adventure.

"Wow. So, did you do it? Did you get the sample?"

He gave me a cocky grin.

"Of course I did."

The commander obviously hadn't experienced failure in his life very often. Having to give up the abducted human women had been hard for him to do. I wondered what made him do it at the end.

"How about the hostile locals?" I asked.

"The locals weren't my biggest problem. That planet has worms." He grimaced.

"Oh. So do we. We have worms on Earth, too. You dislike worms that much?" I lifted my eyebrows in surprise.

He threw a cautious glance around.

"How big are the worms on Earth? I don't remember."

"Like this. About." I lifted my pointer fingers in the air with a few inches between them.

"In diameter?"

"What? No!" I shook my head, laughing. "A worm that thick? That would be a nightmare."

"The worms on the mountain of Varae are as thick as I'm tall and as long as this tree is high." He pointed at a massive long-leaf pine nearby.

"No way!" I tilted my head all the way back to see the top of the tree swaying in the breeze high up. "That's insane."

"The worms aren't just big, they're also incredibly vicious and bloodthirsty. They're always hungry, too. When a worm smells its victim, it shoots out its jaw, which opens like a net, set with teeth that can pulverize rock. The net traps the prey, and the teeth shred it to pieces for the worm to ingest."

My eyes open wide, I listened, enthralled, suspended between repulsion and awe.

"Wow. Did you actually get to see that?"

"Once." He nodded slowly. "Not a pleasant sight, but at that moment I was glad the prey was a local animal and not me."

"Has a worm like that ever attacked you?" I asked with slight trepidation.

"Twice. Once on the way there, another time on the way back."

"I can't imagine what that must've been like. How did you survive?"

He leaned on his arm propped against the log.

"The trick is to fight it from behind and stay away from its jaw in the front. The worm can only project it forward, not backward. That's all." He shrugged with easy confidence.

"Sounds simple!" I laughed out loud, slapping my thighs.

He watched me, a slight smile playing on his lips. The intensity in his eyes flustered me, my laughter trailing off.

I blinked, jerking my gaze away, and tucked a strand of my hair behind my ear.

"And now you withdraw again," he muttered, sounding disappointed.

"What do you mean?" I asked, not meeting his eyes.

"You're like the *iechai* shell, Lori," he said in a soft, enthralling voice. "It has a neat, polished outer surface that blends well with the environment. Only when the *iechai* feels safe and comfortable does it open, allowing a glimpse of the magnificent, golden pearl inside. As soon as it senses but the slightest threat, it snaps closed again."

I'd been told similar things before, though nothing this poetic and only by people who'd known me for much longer than the commander had.

It normally took me a painfully long time before I started feeling myself around a new person—the reason I never sought new acquaintances. Dating or making new friends always came with a hefty share of awkwardness for me.

"You're very perceptive, Commander," was all I could manage, momentarily lost for words.

"Lately," he said in the same low, contemplating voice. "I find myself living just for those beautiful glimpses of your soul, Lori. The pieces of your true self."

Stunned, I couldn't say a word in reply. What would one even say to something like that? I'd never had anyone speak this way to me before.

Swallowing hard, I committed every single one of his words to memory. When he was no longer there, I would take them out and admire each, one by one. Alone. Like a miser with a chest full of treasure.

Chapter 12

Lori

"Filthy, blood-sucking monsters!" The commander slapped his neck, releasing an even longer string of curses.

My translator didn't catch that last one, or maybe the poor device just gave up, reaching the limit of alien curses it could translate.

"I'd rather fight a horde of Varae worms!" the commander raged. "At least I can see them coming. These bugs here are the worst."

"Mosquitos are vicious and annoying around here," I sympathized.

We'd warmed up the ravioli I'd brought with me for dinner, and now were having some early blueberries I'd found nearby for dessert. Most of them were still largely green, though. It wasn't the season for blueberries yet.

The commander rubbed his neck.

"Don't scratch," I warned.

"But it's impossible not to," he groaned.

"Wait, I'll spray you again."

I reached for my backpack for the pump bottle of bug spray. The manufacturer claimed their newest formula was completely harmless and one hundred percent effective, and I had to agree. I'd used a lot of different types of mosquito repellent during my thirty years. So far, this one had proven to be the best. I also loved its flowery lavender smell.

"It's a good spray, but it wears off after a few hours," I told the commander. "It works well while it lasts, though. And it smells good," I added with a smile.

The commander quickly shrugged the Snuggie off, then pulled off the shirt of his uniform over his head. His hands went for the silver clip of the closure on his pants.

"Um… The spray can go on your clothes, you know." I stopped him as he was about to yank his pants down his legs. "You don't need to *disrobe*."

Not that I minded watching him taking his clothes off. The problem was I liked it way too much.

At first, the commander had been cautious and guarded around me. When I'd treated his bug bites last night, he'd acted playful and even flirty. Today, there was something poignant and slightly wistful about him.

Intentionally or not, he'd been showing me the many sides of himself, and so far, I appreciated them all, which was…troubling. I'd never met anyone whom I'd liked so thoroughly and completely. What did this mean, now? And where could it lead?

He waited for me, standing in his half-naked, plum-purple glory.

"But last time, I had no clothes on when you sprayed me," he pointed out.

Was he disappointed that I didn't let him get naked?

"Last night, you already had your clothes off when I found you, remember?" I handed him the spray bottle. "Here, do your front. Don't forget to close your eyes and hold your breath. This formula has been proven completely harmless—finally, they've come up with something that repels mosquitoes without harming people. But you still don't want to breathe the liquid in."

"Right." Closing his eyes, he sprayed his chest with a generous amount of the repellent from the bottle.

The moment he finished, I gaped at him with my mouth wide open. His dark gray-purple skin was normally the color the sky took sometimes right after the sunset. Now it glowed iridescent blue and green wherever the spray had hit it. His arms and chest appeared as if covered with stars in a shimmering mist.

"What is that?" He stretched his left hand in front of him, examining his arm closely.

"It didn't do it last night, did it?" I certainly didn't remember him glowing.

He turned his arm, studying the glow. "Maybe that's the effect of the second layer? It glows where the spay is layered on top of the one from yesterday."

It must be that, in combination with something in his skin.

"You're glowing in the dark. So bright." I kept staring at him. "It's really beautiful."

"I don't think anyone has ever called me beautiful before." He huffed a laugh.

Mesmerized, I couldn't take my eyes off him. The glow highlighted the dips and valleys of the well-defined landscape of his torso. Fine droplets of spray had hit his face. His high cheekbones now appeared dusted by tiny stars.

"You look like a night sky, sprinkled with magic," I breathed out.

He caught my gaze, and the amused smile slipped off his face. He took a step closer, then another one, stepping softly like a predator in the woods.

I halted my breath, but didn't back off. Instead, I searched for something to say, anything to break this charged silence that descended between us.

"That's a weird reaction to the spray," I mumbled when his chest was but a few inches away from my face. "How are you feeling?"

I ventured to glance up at his face dusted with starlight. His lavender eyes glimmered in the night, like two stars on their own. He was truly beautiful. Strong and powerful. An out-of-this-world miracle who had descended from the stars to stand here in the woods with me.

To spend one last night together.

"No one has ever looked at me the way you do, Lori. With wonder and admiration," he murmured. "It makes me want to be the man you think I am."

"There is a lot to be admired about you, Commander." His appearance and attitude might've attracted my attention first, but the more I got to know him, the more things I discovered to appreciate.

I loved his protectiveness of me. Here, in the place that was practically my home and where he was a stranger, he still found ways to look after me. All this time, he had been mindful of my needs, from mealtimes to trekking through the woods. I'd called him my bodyguard, but he had proven to be so much more.

Sure, I could take care of myself, but him taking care of me filled my heart with tenderness and appreciation. The feelings rose in my chest, begging to be expressed in some way—any way.

As always, I knew I'd fail if I tried to put it into words. So, I didn't even try. Instead, I lifted my hand, gently touching the glow on his chest.

"Maybe this is a delayed allergic reaction to the spray?" I said, focusing on the subject that felt safe. "Does it hurt at all?"

"No." He leaned to me, so close, his breathing moved the hair on top of my head.

"Any other symptoms?" I asked softly, avoiding his gaze. "Tightness of breath?" I was experiencing that myself, though it had nothing to do with the spray and everything with the man standing so close to me. "Numbness? Stiffness in your neck?"

"Stiffness. Yes." His voice flowed deep and slow over me, like thick, melted caramel warming my skin.

"In your neck?" I shot my gaze up, and it was immediately trapped in the midnight-purple of his eyes. They seemed so much darker now that the sun had set.

His eyelids dropped half-way, and a corner of his mouth lifted in a crooked smile.

"Lower, Lori. The stiffness is much lower than my neck," he murmured, his tails rising behind him.

A burst of heat seemed to set my face on fire. The heat then traveled down my body.

Lower...

As if on its own, my gaze shifted downwards, too. It slid down along the hard ridges of his abdominal muscles, to the belt of his uniform, and...lower, where his *stiffness* pushed urgently against the thin material of his pants.

The commander's breathing grew ragged, yet he wouldn't touch me, keeping just a tiny distance between us.

"You never told me what you wanted to talk to me about, Lori." His nostrils flared as he breathed in. "Why did you approach me, back on the Conqueror?"

Oh, no... I couldn't talk to him about that without revealing my feelings for him, the feelings that had grown far past a mere crush or infatuation by now. I couldn't handle that conversation, not with him half-naked standing this close to me.

"At this point, I'd rather you think me a spy." I managed a smile.

He chuckled.

"I never truly believed you were a spy, sweetheart. I just tried very hard to convince myself that you were."

"Why?" My heart fluttered with sweet pleasure from the word of endearment he'd just used. Said in that deep voice of his, the effect of it was nearly physical. *"Sweetheart"* stroked something so deep inside me, it was in a place that no one could reach before him.

"I hoped convincing myself you were a spy would serve as a restraint in keeping me away from you," he explained.

Was that what I'd been trying to do, too? I'd never even asked for his name because in my mind, addressing him by his rank helped keeping the distance between us.

"It was stupid of me." He exhaled a self-deprecating laugh. "The last thing I want is to be away from you. Tell me, what did you want to talk to me about?" he demanded in that tone of authority that made me weak in my knees and was impossible to disobey.

I swallowed hard and confessed, "I hoped to invite you here. To spend the weekend with me."

His tails curved, caging us from both sides without touching.

"What did you plan to do if I accepted?" he insisted.

I released a brief laugh charged with nerves.

"I never went that far in my fantasies," I admitted.

"I did," he declared unexpectedly.

My breath hitched.

"You...fantasized about us?"

He licked his lips, giving me a lazy smile.

"That's all I've been doing lately, Lori. From the moment I saw that blush..." The tip of one of his tails stroked my cheek—a tender caress, like a brush of a finger, "I've wondered what your skin would feel like to touch." Another stroke of his tail—down my neck, this time. "To kiss." A caress down my chest, all the way to my cleavage in the opening of my shirt. "To lick," he finished in nearly a whisper.

Other than that one point of contact, our bodies didn't touch anywhere else. Yet we were so close, our heat mingled between us, charging the air with energy and tension.

"Every minute since," the commander continued in a husky voice. "I've imagined what you'd look like with your legs spread open for me. What you'd taste like. I went through every position I'd love to have you in, and I keep coming up with more."

Heat coursed through me, making me unsteady on my feet. Trembling, I shut my eyes, letting my head drop. My forehead leaned against his chest.

"The things I would do to you if you were mine," he growled.

I couldn't take it anymore—this overwhelming need for him.

"Let's pretend that I am," I said in a half-whisper. "For one night, let's pretend that I'm yours."

Unable to resist any longer, I took that one tiny step, closing the distance between us.

His tails whipped around me, binding me and claiming me for him. He wrapped his arms around me, too.

Air rushed out of my chest, and my knees buckled. He held me tight, though, not letting me fall.

Pressing a side of his face to my head, he went still for a second.

"Holding you feels even better that I've imagined," he purred above my ear.

Sliding a hand up my back and neck, he speared his fingers through my hair, breaking the elastic band that held my ponytail. My wavy, chestnut hair fell freely down my shoulders. The commander raked his fingers through it, grabbing handfuls of it, then letting it go.

"This feels fantastic," he murmured, burying his face in my hair. "It smells like you."

I smiled, enjoying every moment of his affection. This must be the first time the commander got to play with hair since Ivodians didn't have any.

He cupped the back of my neck, caressing my skin.

"Clothes. Off," he ordered.

I raised my trembling fingers to the buttons of my shirt, but he caught my hand. "Let me."

He kept my hand in his, but a gentle touch skirted my waist. Another one trailed from around my back to my shirt buttons in the front.

His tails.

Two of them slid under the waistband of my jeans, yanking the button and the zipper open. Two others lifted my shirt up. The commander kept his hands on me—one in my hair, the fingers of the other laced with mine. He let his tails do the work of undressing me. When my shirt and jeans were off, he leaned back, searching my face with his gaze.

"Let me see you," he rasped.

Gently gliding his hands down my shoulders, he slid off my bra straps. Leaning over me, he deftly flicked my bra open.

"You know how to do that?" I gasped in surprise.

He nuzzled the hair over my temple. "It was part of the course I took."

"What course?"

"On how to pleasure a woman." He glided his palms up and down my back, eliciting waves of pleasure rippling along my skin.

"There is a course for that?" I exhaled.

"Mhm," he hummed against the side of my neck, leaving a trail of kisses there. "Every Ivodian man has to take it to be allowed to have a wife. It was updated with information on human women when Earth was approved for abductions."

"They taught you how to open my bra in class?" I blinked, utterly bewildered.

"Among many other things." He gently nipped the shell of my ear. "I know a thousand and seventy-four ways to pleasure a woman from Earth." He let my bra drop to the ground.

Fresh night air teased my exposed skin. My nipples pebbled.

"A thousand..." I could hardly breathe.

Wrapping an arm around my waist, he moved the other one to my chest. Warm and large, his hand covered one of my breasts completely.

"Was... Was there a test, too?" I tried to make a joke, but the tone was wrong. The question came out breathy, with a soft whimper at the end when he gently pinched my nipple.

Two of his tails slid down my legs, taking my pink underwear with them.

The commander leaned back. Arching an eyebrow ridge, he gave me a crooked grin.

"The test is now, sweetheart. Let me know if I make a mistake."

I sucked in a breath with a startled sound as his tails wound around my ankles and yanked. I tilted back, flailing my arms, but didn't fall. The commander let go of my waist, but two other tails replaced his arms, lifting me up.

"You're safe," he assured me, taking a step back. "Now, let me see you."

His tails snaked around me. Two were wound around my ankles, two around my middle. Two others slid up my sides, trapping my arms. Bound hand and foot and tilted back slightly, I was held suspended over the forest floor.

"Yess," he hissed with satisfaction. "I've dreamed about having you, just like this."

I squeaked when his tails yanked my legs apart, fully exposing me to him.

He groaned low. His tails tugged me closer to him. I swayed in the air like in a swing, helpless and burning with anticipation.

The bulge in his pants pressed between my legs. A low rumble resonated deep inside his chest.

He leaned over me.

"That sweet, tantalizing blush," he murmured before kissing my cheek. His lips felt cool against my flushed skin.

I jerked my hand to touch him, but he yanked at his tails, moving my hands above my head.

Not chains but so much stronger, his tails bound me, positioning me for him like a rag doll or a marionette.

"Kiss me," I demanded, turning my face to his. "Touch me, if I can't touch you."

Taking my head in his hands, he lowered his mouth to mine.

"I want to breathe you, taste you, feel you. Everywhere," he whispered between hot, biting kisses as he devoured my mouth. His forked tongue flicked against mine, sending a rush of thrill down my body.

I writhed in my restraints that were softer and gentler than chains but felt so much stronger. Unyielding. There was no escaping this bond. His seventh tail slinked between us, the tip flicking my nipples. Desire flooded me with a tsunami of heat.

"Want you..." I moaned as he trailed his kisses down my body. "So, so much..."

Heat spiraled and curled low in my belly, building in intensity. Bound hand and foot, I could do nothing about it. Straining against the bindings on my ankles, I pressed my core against the bulge in his pants harder.

Sliding his hand between us, he yanked the closure of his pants open. I rubbed myself against his hand in desperation.

"So impatient," he murmured with a smile in his voice. Sliding a finger between my folds, he growled approvingly, finding me hot and sleek.

He moved his finger inside me, kissing my breast. His tongue flickered against my nipple, tantalizing and exciting every nerve in my body.

He released a pained groan.

"I need to get inside you, now. Or I'll lose my mind."

I could only moan in response, feeling like I was losing my mind already. Something hot and blunt pressed against my entrance—the tip of his erection. I jerked in my restraints, breathless with anticipation.

"Come here, my sweet Lori." His tails shifted me closer, impaling me on his hard length.

A slick slide against my most sensitive spot made me tremble. My hips bucked, my eyes open wide. He slid just another inch in, and the same sensation happened again, spiking the pleasure inside me.

"Oh God," I moaned wildly, barely able to hold it together. "It's so, so good. What is it?"

His smile turned smug.

"One of the thousand and seventy-four ways to pleasure you, my beauty."

"They can lick with their dicks." Maddy's words sounded in my mind.

It certainly felt like a lick of a soft yet firm tongue against my swollen clit. Another inch in, and I frantically ground my hips against him, driven wild with need.

The commander thrust harder. His every slide in and out of me was accompanied by the firm, hot "licking" right where I needed him.

The pleasure inside me spiraled out of control and exploded in a myriad of fireworks through every inch of my body.

"I've got you," he said softly, his tails bringing my ankles together behind his back. My legs wrapped around his hips, his tails brought my torso into his arms, releasing my wrists.

I wrapped my arms around his neck, riding the best climax I'd ever had. And he chased his own, frantically pumping his hips into me.

He exhaled a shuddered breath, coming hard inside me. I kept holding on to him. His tails wrapped around both of us, binding us together as if we were one. The glow on his skin illuminated us like starlight.

Intense pleasure slowly receded. Warm, complete happiness filled me as he held me in his arms.

He raked his fingers through my hair, placing a small, tender kiss on the side of my face.

"Chained or not, you belong in my bed, Lori."

His hard, chiseled features softened when he looked at me. The night in his eyes was tender and warm.

I traced the row of his piercings from his nose up his forehead to almost the middle of his head. He squinted with a smile, then caught my hand and kissed it.

"What's your name, Commander Nex?" I asked. "Do you have a first name?"

"I do. It's Brigan. Brigan Nex," he said.

Brigan...

It suited him.

No longer just "the commander" to me, he felt closer, dearer, harder to part with. Just like I'd feared he'd be.

Tenderness for him pinched my heart with ache and sweetness. My arms wrapped tightly around him, I leaned my head to his.

"I really, really like you, Brigan."

He stroked my hair, combing with his fingers through it. His tails slacked around us, draping loosely. I wished we could stay like this forever, illuminated only by the glow of his skin and the light of the stars above.

"Come, Lori," he said, heading toward our tent. "There're still so many ways I can make you scream in pleasure, and the night is short."

"Brigan..." I murmured, snuggling closer to him in his arms.

The night ahead did seem impossibly short.

Chapter 13

Brigan

Lori murmured something in her sleep. He'd kept her up well into the night, making love to her in so many delightful ways. He hadn't wanted to stop. He couldn't get enough of her. But he had taken her so many times, both of them had ended up exhausted, falling asleep just like they were, wrapped in each other's arms and his tails.

This morning, he woke up with her head resting on his chest, her soft hair tickling his skin. The warmth of Lori's naked body seeped into his.

The thin, whiny sounds of the flying bugs reached him, but the insects weren't biting. The spray must be working again, though the bizarre glowing of his skin was now gone without a trace.

Gray light filtered through the orange material of the tent. The night had ended, and it hurt him to think about it. He had to say good-bye to her soon. But he just couldn't...

Lori was his.

She belonged with him.

He kissed her shoulder, and she moaned, her eyes closed. He kept kissing, needing to hear more of her moans.

Her skin smelled like fresh air, the long needles of the trees in this forest, and the flowery scent of the spray that kept the nasty flying bugs away. She smelled like this getaway, the best trip of his entire life.

He rolled her over and sucked the tip of her breast in his mouth. The course had taught him that human women generally liked it when a man paid attention to their breasts, especially the tips. He knew for sure now that Lori liked it, too. Her nipples were still red and hot after all the attention he'd paid to them through the night.

By now, he could write a course of his own—a course on how to make love to Lori in ways that would make her scream his name over and over again. At the same time, there was so much more he still wanted to learn about her.

Closing his teeth around her nipple, he gently rolled it between them, squeezing just enough to make her gasp.

"Comm... Brigan?" she murmured, stretching through the entire length of her body.

He let the nipple pop out of his mouth, then he slid lower.

"What time is it?" she asked sleepily.

He flicked her nipples with his tails while parting her legs.

"Time to taste you, my dear," he chuckled softly.

The little sensitive bud between her folds fit perfectly in the fork of his tongue. They were simply made for each other.

She squeaked when he licked, then tried to jerk her legs back together. He wound a tail around each of her thighs, gently but firmly holding them apart. There were ways to make her come even with her legs closed, but he was feeling selfish this morning. He wished to have her open to him fully and completely, like a flower. He wanted to taste every sacred part of her.

Holding her legs apart with his tails, he flicked his tongue against the spot that made her whimper with pleasure. He kept licking and sucking until her whimpers turned to loud moans.

"Brigan..." she panted.

The sound of his name from her lips, said in that breathy voice of hers between moans of pleasure, made his cock hard like a rock. Every petal on it swelled hot and thick.

He groaned, sucking harder.

Lori's moaning broke off. Her breathing halted, then erupted into a series of tortured little gasps as she came hard on his tongue. He held her hips, licking every little shudder out of her, milking her climax for as long as he could to give her the most pleasure.

"Oh, what a way to wake up..." she exhaled finally.

Her body slaked in the loops of his tails. He rose on his outstretched arms.

"Good morning." She squinted sleepily with a languid smile. "A glorious morning, I shall say." A soft giggle left her lips, and he loved the sound of it—cute and girlish.

He pulled himself up her body and rolled to his side next to her. His cock ached, pulsing with strain. But he could just lay with her like this forever, as long as she kept smiling at him like that.

She lifted her hand to his face.

"What are these piercings for? Do they mean anything?" She touched the horizontal crescents of his insignia inserted through the skin high on his face and up his head.

Touching them casually like that was not permitted on Ivodi. Lori's little finger trailing along them added a salacious feeling of breaking a taboo. He was enjoying her touch way too much to even think about stopping her.

Instead, he took her hand in his, moving it for her.

He pressed the tip of her finger to the first crescent on the bridge of his nose. "My current rank." He moved it higher, to the one above the first one. "The rank I held before it." He kept going. "My most successful mission. The first ship I flew on. The school I attended. The town where I was born."

"How about this one?" she asked when they made it all the way up to the highest placed crescent on his scalp.

"This one says 'Nex.'" He slid her finger along his family name engraved on the smooth surface.

"It's the most important one, isn't it?" She must've paid attention to the Ivodian salute during her trips to the Conqueror.

He nodded, releasing her hand. She dropped it between them, and he immediately recaptured it again, lacing his fingers with hers.

"The top crescent represents everything an Ivodian man holds dear—his family, his heart, and his honor," he said.

"Your warriors touched that one when they saluted you." She proved very observant.

He nodded. Sense of pride warmed his chest. "That's the sign of highest respect."

"You touched this one when greeting me." She tapped the bottom piercing in line.

"That's customary when greeting foreigners and strangers, especially for work or during a mission."

She arched one of her delicate brow ridges. Typical for humans, it had a strip of short dark hairs running along it. He itched to touch it.

"Strangers?" she asked. "But I'm no longer a stranger to you, am I?"

"No. Of course not." He smiled.

Giving in to the impulse, he slid the tip of his finger along her brow. The hair there proved silky, but not as soft as the hair on her head. His thoughts then flashed to the hair between her legs, and his erection bobbed with a new surge of lust.

"So, if I'm no longer a stranger, what would you touch now when you see me?" Lori asked innocently.

He grinned with glee.

"This." He reached behind her and grabbed a handful of her delectable ass, making her squeak. "And this." He skimmed her breast, then sank his hand into her hair on the back of her head. "All of this." He scooped her in his arms and slunk all his tails around her.

She fit so well in his embrace. She was made for him.

Lori laughed softly against his mouth as he placed a kiss on her lips.

"But what are these?" she asked when he let her come up for air.

Her delicate fingers skimmed along the row of slim locators implanted in his skin—five of them on each side of his head, just above his temples. He wasn't sure he wanted to talk about them, sensing it might stir their conversation into the area he'd rather avoid. This morning proved too enjoyable to spoil it.

"Do these toothpicks mean anything?" she insisted.

"Toothpicks?" he chuckled.

"Well, what are they?"

The touch of her fingers sent shivers of pleasure down his spine. He couldn't deny her.

"These are locators," he explained with a sigh. "If I break one, it'll send a distress signal to the Conqueror. A shuttle then would come pick me up."

The locators were implanted in his skin on his head because luggage could be taken, clothing could be destroyed, and limbs could be lost in battle. Activating a locator was the last resort when everything else had failed and the only solution remained was to retreat.

It was a symbol of failure and defeat in his eyes. Ivodians never failed.

Her large gray eyes grew larger as she shrank back from him.

"You mean you could've called for help all this time? That easily? And you haven't done it yet?"

He'd never used a locator in his entire life. He most definitely was not going to use one now.

"I'll get back to my ship on my own," he said resolutely.

A shadow moved over her expression.

"Because you don't want the others to see me with you," she stated softly.

As he'd feared, the conversation turned to the topic he didn't want to discuss—parting from her.

"Not yet," he said.

Her gaze shot to his. The hope in her eyes floored him. She didn't want to part from him, either. Triumph filled his chest, as if he'd just won the biggest, most important battle in his life.

He could lie to himself all he wanted, but he couldn't leave her. Lori belonged with him. He simply needed to find a way to make it happen.

"Not yet?" she repeated, looking at him expectantly.

He shook his head and cupped her face.

"This can't be it." Now that he'd had her, tasted her, owned her, one night wasn't enough. He needed her for life.

A wide smile spread across her lips.

"No, Brigan, this can't be it," she echoed.

The sound of his name from her mouth intensified the throbbing in his cock. His hips involuntarily rocked into hers. She bit her lip, that lovely blush of hers making an appearance.

Sliding one of his tails down her thigh, he wound it around her knee, bringing her leg up and over his hip. The row of erect petals along his cock rubbed against her sex.

She sucked in a shuddered breath.

"Oh, God... What is that? I need to see it." She leaned back, reaching down with her hand.

"You haven't seen an Ivodian cock yet," he grinned smugly. It was universally acknowledged that Ivodians had the best equipment in that department.

"No," she laughed. "I haven't *seen* it, though it spent a large chunk of the night inside me."

His erection throbbed harder at her words. Clearly, his member yearned to be back inside her again.

She took him in her light, delicate fingers. He moaned, tossing his head back when she ran her thumb over his swollen petals. Desire pulsed through his entire body, hot and urgent.

"These are the 'tongues' that do all that licking..." she murmured, stroking him nearly into oblivion from pleasure of her touch.

"Tongues?" he panted, struggling not to explode into her hand.

"Mhm. Like mine. See?" She stuck her blunt, pink tongue out. He couldn't resist trying to catch it in a kiss. She laughed, withdrawing her tongue quickly, and he kissed her smiling lips instead.

The seven petals lined up on the top of his cock looked nothing like his slim, forked tongue. But they were very similar to Lori's. When he wasn't aroused, they lay flat against his shaft, like flower petals in a bud. When he was hard, like he was right now, they swelled and rose. Not as hard as his cock, they were firm enough to rub against that sensitive bud atop Lori's entrance when he thrust inside her.

He remembered the wild moans she made when he took her last night. He had to hear them again.

Rolling her on her back, he fitted himself between her legs.

"Let me show you my "cock tongues" in action again," he growled, pushing inside her.

"Oh God, yes..." She released a long breath, arching her back, her body so soft and pliable in his hands.

He thrust harder, and the world fell apart.

Only she remained. Lori and him. Just the two of them in the entire Universe.

Chapter 14

Brigan

"Breakfast time." Sticking her feet out of the shelter, Lori put her sturdy hiking boots on, then climbed out. "You'll make the fire while I'll catch a fish for us. Deal?"

All they had left for food were a couple of Lori's little ration bars she called "granola." He didn't worry about being able to provide for her in this area, though. There were plenty of animals around. With the weapon that Lori brought with her—as primitive as it was—he wouldn't even have to chase or wrestle a prey.

Fish would be the easiest, since the river was right there. But she wanted to do it herself.

"How will you catch it?" he asked, curious and not a little worried.

They had no fishing rods, but he could catch a fish with his hands and tails if he had to. The high, foamy rapids in this part of the river would make it challenging, but not impossible. He wondered how this human woman was intending to accomplish it, without having one single tail on her.

"With this!" She grabbed a small pouch from her backpack, then produced a silver reel with a thin clear line from it. "Unless we went fishing near the cabin, Grandpa never carried a rod with him. He used to say, 'A stick is the easiest thing to find in the woods. Why would I schlep one with me?' He scoffed when I suggested a telescopic rod to him."

Chatting, she searched around her, then picked up a short stick off the ground and clipped the reel to the middle of it.

"I don't need to cast here. The rapids will carry the hook for me," she explained. "I'll just have to climb out there and watch that it doesn't get stuck in the rocks. There's plenty of trout around here. Bet I'll catch one before you'll even make a fire," she teased, heading for the river.

He fought the intense urge to stop her.

Instinct pressed him to keep Lori in the safety of the tent while *he* provided food for their breakfast. He fought his instincts fiercely only out of respect for her and her culture.

Lori wasn't an Ivodian. Human women weren't generally as sheltered. He sensed she would not appreciate him restricting her activities or doubting her abilities again.

That didn't mean he could just go about his business calmly, leaving her to her own devices. He watched her furtively while building the fire, making sure she was okay.

Lori had proven herself a capable woman. It thrilled him to see her confidently hop from rock to rock between the rapids. White water rushed around her ankles, spraying the bottoms of her blue pants. She spread her feet wide for balance. Adjusting the lure, she threw the hook as far as she could. The stream caught it, and she let the line unfurl from the reel. Holding the stick with the line in one hand, she moved the other arm away from her body for balance.

He took in her figure, small but strong and capable. She would fit perfectly into the lifestyle he envisioned for himself on Us'ae. His land there was more mountainous than this area. But there were also rivers, a big lake, and plenty of fish.

He could see spending days like this with Lori. The two of them hiking under the tall blue trees on his property. Catching rainbow colored fish in the milky streams. Sleeping in a lightweight shelter pitched under the stars. Making love whenever they felt like it.

With Lori, he would never be torn between going for a hike or staying home with his wife. They'd go together. Everywhere.

All he had to do was to make Lori his wife.

The idea of that warmed his heart. It felt so right. She was born to be with him. He sensed it.

A plan started forming in his head. He would have to say goodbye to her, but only temporarily. There was no way he'd part with Lori for good. Her heart and spirit had captured him even before he'd claimed her body.

He'd take her to her cabin, then find his way back to his ship. Before the Conqueror would leave Earth, his crew would do their final round of abductions, grabbing the ninety-seven women they'd come here for. Lori would be bride number ninety-eight.

With Lori at his side, he didn't mind retiring now rather than years later as he'd planned. Lori was worth giving up that. He wouldn't leave this planet without her. She had to come with him.

"Got one!" Her excited voice rose over the noise of the rushing water.

She flashed him a smile over her shoulder. One eyebrow arched high, giving her a cheeky expression. He wished he could kiss that smile and that face right now.

Her line stretched tight like a string, forcing her to jump on the rocks further down the stream to follow the fish she'd caught. "It's a big one!"

Worry rose higher the further away she moved from him. Dropping the lighter he was about to use to start the fire, he straightened to his full height. Every muscle in his body flexed, ready to jump to her help if needed.

The fish was obviously big, yanking at the line in a fight for its life. And Lori had nothing but uneven, slippery rocks for footing. The rapid water was trying to knock her over with every step.

She shifted her position for better balance. The fish yanked again. Lori grabbed on to the stick with both hands, bracing her feet. A short log bounced down the stream with the rapids. Her attention absorbed by the struggling fish, Lori didn't see it heading her way.

"Behind you!" he yelled in warning.

She jerked her head back, glancing upstream over her shoulder. The fish yanked again, stronger than before. Her left boot slipped off the rock she was standing on. Her leg went into the water up to her hip and under a large rock upstream.

"Lori!"

He ran.

Not fast enough.

Pushed by the stream, the rock rolled on Lori's leg, knocking her over. She had no chance to scream. Water rushed over her in lacy, white swells, taking her under.

His deafening roar drowned the noise of the rapids as he launched across the stream to her. In two huge leaps, he was at her side.

She fought the torrent. Her head popped up, her mouth open and gasping for air.

He grabbed under her arms, lifting her head above the water.

She screamed in agony when he tried to take her in his arms.

Frantically, he searched with his tails under water around her body. The rock had crushed her leg, trapping her.

He cradled her head with his tails, holding it above water so she could breathe. Filling his lungs with air in one gulping breath, he dove under.

Churning, white water blinded him when he tried to open his eyes. He felt his way down her body toward the massive rock trapping her leg from above her knee down.

With his feet, he found a couple of stable rocks and propped his boots on them. Pressing his shoulder into the rock that held Lori captive, he shoved at it with all his might. The rock gave under his power. He rolled it off Lori's leg, then let the river carry it down the stream a few paces further.

The water caught Lori, trying to pry her away from him. Looping his tails around her, he wouldn't let her go.

Pulling her closer, he took her in his arms. His tails cradled her leg like a sling.

"Lori?"

She was so pale, she looked like a bloodless creature of the river herself. Water sluiced down her face, droplets caught in her eyelashes. Her blue-gray eyes open wide, she gave him a faint smile.

"He got away," she said apologetically.

It took him a moment to realize she was talking about the damn fish.

"Fuck him," he gritted through his teeth, plowing through the water toward the shore.

He already knew her leg was in bad shape. It dangled limply in the coils of his tails, providing no resistance when jolted. The blue material of her pants quickly soaked with red before the river water even had a chance to recede.

"You'll be okay, Lori," he said firmly to reassure both her and himself.

"I'm so, so sorry, Brigan. My foot slipped and knocked out a rock that must've supported that big one," she chatted energetically, despite her condition. Clearly, the pain hasn't fully registered yet. "I let the fish go. Nearly drowned myself. What a mess." She shook her head. "It's never happened to me before."

He placed her on the patch of moss by the fire he'd never started. Trying to get her into the tent would only aggravate her leg.

"Thank you for getting me out of there. Are you okay?" she asked, as if *he* were the one injured.

"I'm fine." He reached for the sheathed knife nearby.

She studied his face, trembling slightly. Shock must be setting in already. He'd seen enough injuries in his life to read the signs easily. Humans and Ivodians weren't that different after all.

"Brigan..." She winced.

"It hurts. I know." He slid the knife out of the sheath.

"A little," she groaned softly. "We'll need to make a splint and find something I could use for a crutch. I'll be hopping all the way to the cabin from here." She managed a smile that didn't last long.

He made his tails lower her leg to the ground as gently as he could. Still, it wasn't gently enough.

She gritted her teeth, choking on a groan of pain.

By the odd angle of her foot to her leg, he knew she had broken bones. He just needed to get a better idea of how bad it was. Grabbing the end of her pant leg, he cut the material open from her ankle to her thigh.

She sucked in a breath.

His heart nearly skidded to a stop at the sight of her leg. A silent scream stuck in his throat. He choked it down, terrified of freaking her out.

Her bone was clearly shattered. Fragments of it broke through the muscle and skin in three places, marring her smooth skin with thick rivulets of blood. The sturdy material of her pants had protected her skin from more damage, but the injury to the muscle and bone was clearly severe.

There was no way to set this. No splint would hold it.

With a trembling hand, Lori brushed aside the wet strands of her hair from her face. Perspiration beaded on her forehead, mixing with remnants of river water.

She stared at her leg in horror.

"I have a radio back at the cabin." She panted in an effort to keep her composure. Her teeth chattered, her trembling growing into full-body shakes. "For emergencies. You'll have to send a distress signal to the RCMP—the local police station..."

Did she think he'd leave her here? Alone?

He'd carry her all the way back to the cabin, but that'd be no good. It would take him several hours to get there, even if he ran all the way without stopping. By the time the local authorities dispatched help and it arrived, infection would start. The little medical kit Lori had on her wasn't nearly enough to sterilize the three deep gashes in her skin and muscles that had been thoroughly soaked in river water.

"Brigan, I'll be fine here," she tried to convince him, even as she could no longer lift her head, lying on the ground where he'd placed her. "Your secret will be safe, too. You won't have to tell them who you are. You don't even have to speak..." Her hard, shallow breathing was robbing her of words. She spoke between gasps for air. "Once you get to the cabin, send the distress code...and leave the map with my location for them to find... No one will know...that you were here."

Even in this grave condition, she worried about *him*.

The moss under her was quickly soaked with blood. She was losing too much of it, which told him some large blood vessels must've been punctured in her leg. He wrapped one of his tails tightly around her leg, high on her thigh, to stop the bleeding, but every minute of delay could be crucial.

Even if he got her to a medical facility in time, he feared humans simply weren't medically and technologically advanced enough to provide adequate care for her. They wouldn't be able to heal completely an injury this grave. Even if Lori survived, she might never have a full use of her leg again.

"I'll be fine..." she assured him softly.

He nodded.

"Yes, you will."

There was but one thing to do.

He lifted his hand to the row of locators on the side of his head.

Her eyes grew wider. Shock overshadowed the pain in them.

"No... Brigan, you can't..." Tears glistened in her eyes, mixing with the droplets of river water on her eyelashes. "You'll lose everything..."

He didn't give a fuck about that. Nothing was important anymore.

"Nothing is worth losing you."

He pressed the middle of one of the locator capsules. Hard. The device was not designed to break easily. The vibration resonated through his skull when it snapped.

She closed her eyes tightly. Tears streamed down the sides of her face, and he knew these were not just from pain.

"What have you done?" she sobbed. "What will happen to you now?"

It was his turn to lie. "I'll be fine."

He got that funny-but-practical blanket from their tent and tucked it all around her shaking body.

"You'll be okay, Lori." He cradled her head in his lap, wishing he could take her pain, that he could feel it instead of her. "They'll be here in twenty minutes. We will fix your leg. And you will come back here again, healthy and happy. You will be able to hike and fish, to hunt and camp for as long as you want."

"I don't want to do any of that...without you," she groaned.

Would he ever be able to come to this planet again? Would she still want him if he did? Dishonored, with no wealth and no right to marry until he earned it back over a decade or longer?

He held her. He wiped the sweat off her forehead and the tears off her cheeks. And he whispered soothing words into her ear.

A silver disk of the Ivodian shuttle hovered over the treetops—its shape unmistakable, nothing like any aircraft found on Earth. The shuttles of the Conqueror were as fast as its medical chambers efficient. Nothing was more important than keeping his warriors safe and healthy.

"You'll feel better soon," he whispered to Lori.

She didn't open her eyes, either exhausted or passed out from pain.

Carefully, he took her in his arms again, slinking his tails gingerly around her leg.

A wide ray of green light descended from the middle of the silver disk above. A figure hovered inside it.

"Commander Nex. Glad to find you well." The captain of the shuttle saluted him. "We're ready to board. Will it be one person or two?" The male slid a glance at Lori in his arms.

"Two." He rose to his feet carefully, holding Lori close to his chest. "I'll need the medical chamber ready right away, too, Captain."

The pilot slid back up the column of light and disappeared inside the rounded middle of the disk. The beam scooped up Lori and Brigan, lifting them to the center of the shuttle.

He kissed Lori's forehead while ascending the transporting ray of light, whispering against her chilled skin.

"You'll be fine, sweetheart. I'll make sure of it. Even if it's the last thing I do."

Chapter 15

Lori

"Time to wake up, Captain Soranno," a pleasant female voice said in English. The mechanical note in it sounded like an AI. A robot.

How did a robot get to my grandpa's cabin?

I drew in a lungful of air. Clean, breathable, fragrance-free air.

No scent of moss or pine needles. No freshness of the river.

The river.

The rapids and rocks around the waterfall.

My happy place had nearly killed me. I would've drowned had it not been for the commander.

Brigan...

I opened my eyes, greeted by darkness.

The darkness slowly receded, however, replaced by soft, yellow light.

I lay in a bed in a large room of black and silver. The construction of the place followed fluid smooth lines, typical for the interiors of ships and aircraft. It didn't look like anything I'd seen before, though.

The entire wall to my left was a night sky filled with stars...the Earth among them. The huge, brilliant blue disk of my home planet greeted me through the giant window. I was in space, on a ship orbiting Earth.

"Welcome to the Conqueror," the same mechanical voice said.

"Where is Brigan?" I rasped, my throat dry. "Commander Nex?"

"The commander has been notified that you have awakened," the machine replied impassively.

"Where is he?"

"Fulfilling his duties."

As if that explained anything.

I propped my hands on the cushioned surface under me and sat up. I had a weird silver garment on. Loose and comfortable, it was soft like silk but with a metallic shine. The entire thing seemed to be held together with only one flexible clasp on my left shoulder.

The bed was massive. Its black, silky bedding with silver stitching felt luxurious. Several long, thick neckrolls served as pillows. Two of them were propped under a plastic cylinder enclosing my left leg.

"There is a glass of water on the table to your right," the AI voice sounded again.

I glanced to my right. A silver table, in the same smooth, sleek style as the rest of the room, stood next to the bed, with a glass shaped like an inverted cone on it. I shifted closer, reaching for it.

"Please, do not attempt to get out of bed," the AI warned. "You're recovering post-surgery."

Drinking from the cone-shaped glass, I stared at the white contraption on my left leg. It was about a foot in diameter but appeared lightweight like a kite. The plastic material was stretched over a thin-ribbed frame.

I felt nothing below my left hip. No pain. No sensation whatsoever. As if the leg wasn't there at all.

Had I lost my leg?

I set the glass back on the table, struggling to keep my trembling hand steady, and leaned against the pile of cushy neckrolls behind me, shutting my eyes. I remembered Brigan carrying me out of the river. He'd then cut my jeans, exposing my injuries.

The images of mangled flesh, torn skin, and pieces of bone sticking out flashed through my mind. A truly horrific picture. If they hadn't been able to save my leg, it wouldn't be surprising.

Horror caught my breath, seizing my chest so tight it hurt.

"Lori!" the familiar deep voice broke through the darkness that threatened to suffocate me.

"Brigan?" I opened my eyes, searching for him.

The room was disappointingly empty.

"Where are you?" I willed my voice not to shake. The need to see him overwhelmed all my senses, shoving even the darkness aside.

"I'm on my way."

A minute later, a panel in the wall opposite of the bed slid aside, and my commander rushed in.

"I'm here." He clipped the disk of the communication device back to his upper arm, then rushed to me and kneeled at my side. "Lori, my life."

Fresh, crisp, white uniform. Not a trace of the mosquito bites left on his skin—the darkest shade of purple. He looked like nothing had happened at all. Except for his expression. The concern and tenderness in his eyes were the same I remembered from back in the woods.

"How are you feeling, my life?" He stroked my face so gently, the caress melted my heart, bringing tears to my eyes.

Words filled my chest, the most beautiful, wonderful words of gratitude for him, but I couldn't get any of them out. Emotions seized my throat.

Silently, I wrapped my arms around his neck and buried my nose in the skin just above the collar of his uniform. He smelled like warmth and comfort, and everything I wished for in my life.

He kissed my hair, my face, my lips, then leaned his forehead against mine, heaving a breath.

"Is there anything you need?" he asked softly. "Are you hungry? Thirsty?"

My mouth seemed to have completely dried out again.

"Some water." I nodded, reluctantly letting go of him.

He passed me the glass from the table, then sat on the bed next to me to help me take a drink. Water dislodged the tightness in my throat.

"How are you?" I asked him, giving him the glass back.

He obviously still had his rank and position, but for how long?

"I need to get a medic to see you." He didn't answer my question, reaching for the comm device again. I caught his hand in mine. I wasn't ready to invite the rest of the world into our little bubble yet.

"How long have I been under?" I asked.

"Two full days. It's Thursday, according to your calendar."

His comm device beeped softly. Apparently, people didn't care about my wish to have my commander all to myself for a little while.

"Commander," a male voice said from the comm. "The shuttle from Earth is ready to dock."

Of course. It was Thursday—the day of our scheduled flight. Someone must've filled in for me, flying with Maddy today.

Did I even still have a job?

Not unless someone had notified Starlight about my condition.

Brigan tilted his head toward the device on his arm.

"Allow the docking," he ordered. "The deck supervisor has full control, this time. I won't be coming out to the deck."

"Brigan." I placed my hand on his knee the moment the device finally went silent. "What's happened in the past two days? What have I missed?"

He promptly covered my hand with his.

"The moment we got you on the Conqueror, you had surgery," he said. "They then kept you sedated to let your body heal."

He didn't say what kind of surgery, and I dreaded to ask. I avoided looking at the white cylinder that might or might not contain my leg.

He must've noticed that.

"Lori, you'll be fine." He leaned closer, brushing a strand of hair behind my ear. "One of the things Ivodians are really good at is treating injuries. We have centuries of wars, battles, and dangerous exploration missions behind us." He cupped my face. "You will heal completely. In just three weeks, you'll be able to do all the things you like doing—fishing, hiking, hunting."

"Oh, thank God..." I exhaled. Relief flooded me, rendering me speechless for a moment.

Brigan smiled at me, then kissed the tip of my nose.

"But how about you?" I asked, worry anxiously tugging at my heart again.

He kept smiling, but the spark dulled in his eyes.

"Well..." I prompted when he remained silent. "You're still the commander, aren't you?" I pointed at the insignia of his rank running down his left sleeve.

"For now." He sat back.

"What do you mean? What's going on?"

"The investigation is nearly complete," he replied evasively.

"And? What's going to happen now?"

He remained silent, glancing away, toward the giant window.

"Brigan, please." I took his hand in both of mine. "I'm not a stranger, remember. Please, tell me everything."

He gave me a long look, still not saying a word, then slid his thumb over my knuckles.

"You're not a stranger, Lori," he finally said. "So far from it. You're my everything, my entire life."

"I'm your life?" I smiled, a rush of pleasure heating my face. "You...um, we haven't known each other for that long..." That was my reason speaking. My heart embraced his affection, yearning to repay it with the same and more.

He stroked my bare arms, then pulled me in for a quick kiss.

"I'm an Ivodian, remember?" He broke the kiss, but kept holding my arms. "We don't need long to know how we feel. One look at a woman on the street is often enough for us to know she is the one. The first time I saw your blushing face and heard that first awkward 'hi,' I knew I wanted you for life."

"You tried to detain me." I cocked an eyebrow, thinking back to that crazy day when I ended up snatching him from the Conqueror.

He slicked his tails all around me.

"I wished to keep you. Even as later I tried to convince myself that I couldn't."

I splayed my hand on his wide chest, needing his touch more than I needed air to breathe. "What's going to happen to us now, Brigan?"

He groaned. "I hate to upset you."

"Keeping me in the dark would be more upsetting, trust me."

He heaved a breath.

"The crew think I've abducted you," he finally said.

"Fine." I shrugged. "Let them think that."

I didn't care that it wasn't true. This wasn't even a matter of principle. I was more than happy to play the role of the abducted bride if that helped Brigan in any way.

The concern on his face didn't ease, though. The tips of his tails flicked, sending ripples along their length.

"My abducting you was a natural assumption on their part," he said and added, "before the investigation started."

"And now?" I frowned, his worry seeping through to me, too. "What do they think now?"

"Now, there're some questions."

"Like what?"

He stared at me.

"Like why did I go to your cabin instead of bringing you here, for one."

I leaned back against the cushions, feeling deflated.

"What if we told them you came with me to celebrate my birthday?"

Was that a strong enough reason? Was it believable?

"I've told them something along those lines since it *was* your birthday. An outright lie would be easily detected by the speaking device, however. Even if I wanted to lie to my crew."

"Do you think they believed you?"

He rested his forearms on his knees.

"The vote is this afternoon. We'll see soon enough if they believed me and if they still trust me to lead them."

He drew in another deep breath, hanging his head between his wide shoulders.

"There's more, isn't there?" I sensed the unspoken words.

He turned his head to me.

"You want me to tell you everything?"

"Everything." I said firmly. "No matter how upsetting you think it may be."

He nodded, straightening his back.

"I have an agreement with the Coalition of the Earth's Governments," he said resolutely, as if making a grave confession.

"That's right." It dawned on me. "The agreement to return all abducted women. Which means you can't keep me here."

The Earth had made it clear to Ivodians that abductions wouldn't be tolerated. If I posed as an abducted bride, that would mean a breach of agreement on Brigan's part.

"What if I told the Coalition I didn't mind my abduction?" I asked, desperately clinging to hope. Now that I got him, I couldn't possibly part from him.

Would they leave us alone if I said I wanted to stay? Had any of the women tried that before?

He gave me a humorless smile. He didn't seem to share my hope, but he would tell me why.

"What else aren't you telling me, Brigan? Please say it. I'm not going to judge. I need to fully understand the problem to help you with the solution. I'm a part of this too, remember?"

He flexed his jaw, narrowing his eyes.

"I'm afraid the solution is clear, my life. The Coalition captured my Second-in-Command. They're holding him as the collateral against all abductions by the Ivodians. If I keep you, I'll get him killed."

"What?" Horror speared through me with icy arrows. That changed everything. It no longer mattered what I felt. A man's life was at stake here. "No..." I sucked in a sharp breath, leaning back. "They can't do that."

Could they?

His eyebrow ridges shifted closer together.

"Humans are smart," he said. "They've figured out the only thing that would make me go back on my promise to my men—it's the threat to one of our own."

I clasped my hands together in my lap.

"Will they ever release your Second-in-Command?"

"Our agreement states Friday is his release date, after the last abducted brides have left the Conqueror."

"That's tomorrow."

We both fell silent.

I tried to process what he'd just said, looking at it from the point of view of the Ivodian warriors. They'd worked for years to earn their right to marry. Their commander promised them human brides. They went and got them. Then, he forced them to give them up, because of what the Coalition did. Now, he showed up with "a bride" of his own.

It didn't make Brigan look good at all.

So many things were wrong with this situation. The problem was that if Brigan and I kept up with the pretense that he'd abducted me, his man would die. If we told the truth, Brigan would lose his position and everything that came with that, including the chance for any foreseeable future with me.

We hadn't even had an opportunity to discuss our future, and now we might never get to have it at all.

"What are you going to do?" I asked softly.

His throat bobbed with a swallow.

"I can't let them kill my man." His voice sounded hollow and grim.

I nodded. "You're going to tell them the truth."

There really was no other choice.

"Just enough to satisfy the inquiry. I won't get you in trouble. Don't worry," he assured me.

I waved him off. My own troubles were of no concern right now.

"I'm sorry, Brigan. I started all this mess. And now you have to deal with it..." My voice broke off.

"No," he said firmly, gently touching the side of my face. "Lori, I'm not a victim here. Every conscious minute, I've been making my own decisions. Whatever happens to me today will be a consequence of my own actions. Do not blame yourself."

Still, I was inconsolable.

"Had I just been more careful. Had I not broken my leg..."

He shook his head.

"That was an accident. Accidents aren't always preventable. And they can happen to anyone." He stroked along my cheekbone with his thumb, corners of his mouth twitching up in a smile. "Someday, I'll tell you the story about how I lost one of my tails. You may find it funny. I certainly do."

"What?" I blinked. "You lost a tail? Did you have eight before?"

"No. Always only seven. The medics managed to regenerate this one." He poked a tail between us and wiggled the tip. "Though I don't think it regained its full agility, compared to the rest."

The tail twined higher, then brushed an errant tear off my cheek.

I closed my eyes and drew in a long breath, trying to compose myself.

"When is the hearing?" I asked.

"It's in process. I requested a break to see you when the AI notified me that you woke up."

My eyes flew open.

"You're being questioned, right now?" I gasped.

"Yes."

The comm beeped again.

"They're waiting for you, Commander," a male voice said.

"I need to go." He rose to his feet.

"Wait." I grabbed the end of one of his tails as they slipped off me. "Can I come?"

"No. Lori, you need to rest. You're safe here. I'll get someone to bring your lunch right away, and I'll send a medic over after. You can ask them for anything you wish. As an abducted bride, you have more rights than any one of us here."

"Is that so?" I arched an eyebrow. "The abducted women aren't prisoners?"

"Prisoners?" He frowned. "Of course not. Tradition requires them to stay in their husband's bedroom until they get used to their new surroundings and form a bond with their husband. That's all."

"Is this your bedroom?" The room was way too large and luxurious for a medical unit.

"Yes."

"Am I allowed to leave it?"

"No." He tipped his chin at the white cylinder on my leg. "For medical reasons. You're not strong enough to walk yet."

"Okay." I changed my tactic. "But can Maddy visit me, then? I assume she's one of the crew on the shuttle today."

"Maddy? The first officer?"

I nodded.

He paused in thought for a moment.

"I don't see any harm in delaying the shuttle a little so you could see her," he finally agreed. "I'll make the arrangements."

He headed for the exit.

"Thank you. And...Brigan." I couldn't let him leave just like that.

He turned at the door panel to face me.

"No matter what, you'll always have me, Brigan," I said firmly.

He stared at me in silence for a long moment, visibly calm. Only the ends of his long tails twitched slightly, hovering close to the floor.

"The vote is today, Lori," he replied evenly. "Chances are, as of tomorrow, I'll have no rank and no authority. I'll be starting over, with the most mundane assignment on some obscure planet in the furthest corner of the galaxy. I'll be a nobody."

I clamped my hands together, sitting up straighter.

"I don't care, Brigan." I forced my voice not to shake. I needed my words to come out loud and clear. "I don't need a rank or...any of this." I gestured at the lavish furnishings of the room. "I just want you, wherever you are."

Air left him in an audible breath.

"Lori..." He took a step my way.

"Commander," a firm, female voice sounded through the comm. "Your break is over. If you don't return to the Central Assembly Room immediately, you will be detained for breaking the rules."

He stopped as if having run into a wall. His mouth pressed tight, he jerked his head to the side.

"Mother," he muttered under his breath then said into the comm in his usual, authoritative tone, "I'm on my way, Elder Nex."

Elder Nex? Was that his mother? How was she here? I struggled to make sense of it all.

He put his hand on the sliding panel of the exit from the room.

"Lori, whatever comes, I'll do everything to earn my way back to you," he vowed.

Then he was gone.

I believed that every word he'd said to me was true.

Why did I still have a feeling he hadn't told me everything?

Chapter 16

Lori

As Brigan had promised, one of his crew delivered me lunch a minute after he'd left. The Ivodian who'd brought it placed the tray on a small table that fit over my lap, then looked at me expectantly with his light-purple eyes.

"Anything else, Captain Soranno?" he enquired.

I glanced at the large tray laden with enough food to feed a family of six.

"No, I'm good. It looks delicious. Thank you." I picked up a black utensil in the shape of a blunt harpoon.

"If you need anything at all, just contact the Central Communications. The system is voice activated."

"Um..." I stopped him on his way out. "Do you have any updates on the hearing, by any chance? The one about the commander?"

It hadn't been long since Brigan left, but who knew when the next time would be that I'd get to speak to a live person again.

"The hearing is still ongoing, Captain," the Ivodian replied.

"Is it taking place in the Central Assembly Room?" I remembered Elder Nex mentioned it over Brigan's comm device.

"Yes."

"Where about is it located?" I blinked innocently.

The Ivodian looked slightly puzzled by my interrogation but waved a hand over the matte silver hemisphere by the entrance panel. A greenish hologram appeared in the air between him and me, displaying the floor plan of one of the levels of the Conqueror, by the look of it.

"The Central Assembly Room is here." He pointed at an oval shape in the middle.

A silver dot flashed, indicating the location of Brigan's bedroom on the hologram map. I noted the positions of both.

"Thanks. Any chance you could take me there?" I asked the Ivodian.

His eyebrow ridges rose in surprise.

"Your presence has not been requested." He shook his head.

"What if I just wanted to watch the proceedings?" I insisted.

He shifted from foot to foot, hesitating. His tails whipped unsettled around his ankles.

As an abducted bride, you have more rights than anyone, Brigan had said.

The Ivodian obviously was having a hard time denying me anything. And I intended to take full advantage of that.

"Due to your condition, I can't remove you from the room without permission," he finally said.

"Where would you get that permission?" I asked sweetly.

"From the commander, who would have to consult a medical officer. The current instructions are not to move you unless you ask to be taken to the bathroom. But only if you ask. You don't *have to* use the facility. Your garment will absorb and process all impurities. Do you want to go to the bathroom?" He tilted his head.

"Um, no." I touched the soft material of the sleeveless silver robe I was wearing, wondering how many "impurities" it had soaked up in the past two days.

With a content nod, the Ivodian turned to leave once more.

"Well," I stopped him again. "The commander won't be able to give his permission, since he's in the hearing, will he?"

"No, Captain, he will not," he agreed.

"I will miss the hearing then," I pointed out.

"The proceedings are recorded. You can watch them in their entirety any time you wish," he said helpfully.

Right. I could watch the recordings later, when it would be too late for me to make any difference in their outcome.

I had to find another way to get there, the sooner the better.

"Alright. Thank you for the lunch," I released the man.

He gave me a quick bow before leaving.

Brigan had graciously absolved me of all responsibility for what had happened. I took that as his acceptance of my apology, not as an excuse to remain passive now.

"Whatever happens will be the consequence of my actions," he'd said.

If I did nothing now, the consequence of *my* actions would be just that—nothing.

I had to do something.

"Incoming message from the Central Communications," the room's AI system announced in its pleasant female voice with a cold, mechanical note. "Do you wish to accept, Captain Soranno?"

"Um, sure. Accept," I replied distractedly.

"Captain Soranno," a male voice boomed out of the speakers under the ceiling somewhere. "Incoming communication from the Starlight shuttle from Earth."

"Accept, accept, please." I shifted on the bed eagerly, hoping to hear Maddy's voice next.

"Hey, Lori?" she exclaimed cheerfully.

Relief spread through me. It felt like centuries had passed since I'd spoken to her last.

"Yes, Maddy! I'm so glad to hear your voice. Are you coming over?"

"Well, the good man from the Central Comm told me that I can. Our departure time has been delayed. How are you?"

"Good, good. Listen, is there another shipment of suitcases today?" I asked quickly. It'd be so nice to just chat and catch up, but the time was limited, and I had to get something done.

"Yeah, why? Do you need one?" Her voice grew more guarded. "Do you *need* one?" she asked again, with emphasis this time.

I loved Maddy, she was sharp.

"Yes, please. Could you get it to me?" I took a deliberate pause, giving my next words more weight. "In the *luggage cart,* please."

"Right," she replied slowly. "Sure."

She left the last word hanging between us, either waiting for me to say more or wondering if she should say something herself. We both knew the Security Team was listening, though.

"I'll see you soon?" I urged.

"Right," she repeated.

"Do you know how to get here? I'm in the commander's bedroom."

"Are you, now?" she said, still slowly and with added meaning.

Did she think the commander had "chained" me to his bed? Not that I could explain anything to her over the comm anyway, with Security listening.

"Do you know how to get here?" I asked again.

"I'm sure the new deck supervisor will help me figure that out, the charming man that he is," she cooed, obviously for the benefit of someone who was with her out there.

"Okay. I'll see you soon. Don't forget the suitcase. And *the cart.*"

While waiting for Maddy, I poked around the food on the tray in front of me. Most of the things looked familiar—meat, potatoes, fruits, and vegetables. While in orbit around Earth, the Ivodians were using local supplies. I knew that. I personally had delivered quite a few crates with produce and groceries on my shuttle in the past couple of weeks.

The familiar ingredients had been prepared in new, unfamiliar ways, however. Roasted meat had been skewered with grapes and strawberries. Thinly sliced boiled potatoes were layered in a tall glass dish with custard-like substance and fruit, like a dessert. Flaky fish was served on a sweet cracker, topped with chopped dates and whipped egg whites.

As a result, the flavors were unique—unusual but not all unpleasant. I just wasn't hungry, despite having been kept unconscious for two days. The commander was out there, fighting for his future, while I was sitting here, eating a potato dessert.

It wasn't right.

The sliding door opened, and Maddy marched in, pushing the luggage cart in front of her.

"Hey, you!" She beamed at me.

"Maddy!" I moved the table with food away from my lap.

"How are you doing, girl?" She ran to me.

I hugged her so tight, she grunted.

"It's so, so nice to see you, Maddy," I said, finally releasing her.

"How is the leg?" She studied the white cylinder.

"You know I broke it?"

"Yeah, the management sent me a memo about your absence last Tuesday. I tried to call you."

"Sorry, my phone is probably still back at the cabin." I made a mental note to call my parents as soon as possible. I usually spoke with my mom on Fridays. She'd freak if I didn't pick up tomorrow, without at least a text to explain. "So, someone let Starlight know about my leg, then? What did the memo say?"

"Just some general stuff. I need all the details, now." Maddy demanded, plopping on the bed next to me. "What happened?"

"Like the memo said, I broke my leg." I pointed at the cylinder.

"That I know," she dismissed. "Tell me *how* it happened? Did *he* have anything to do with it?" She frowned, her dark eyes turning even darker.

"Who, he? Oh, no. The commander?" I shuddered to think Maddy would even consider Brigan hurting me in any way. "He had nothing to do with it."

She darted a quick look around.

"Are we busting you out?" she asked, lowering her voice.

She yanked the doors of the luggage cart open and tossed the lone suitcase out.

"Let's do it then," she said, looking all business.

One thing for sure, if I ever planned a bank robbery or even a murder, I'd want this woman with me. There simply was no better partner in crime out there.

"That's not what I need the cart for, Maddy." I couldn't help a smile at her eagerness. "The commander has been nothing but kind to me. He saved my life. I'm not planning to escape."

She straightened out, staring at me.

"No? But what's the cart for, then?" Understanding flashed in her eyes, mixed with excitement. "Ooh, are we abducting someone again? Can we grab the new deck supervisor, too?"

"What?" I blinked, trying to catch up with the crazy train of Maddy's thought process. "Why?"

"Have you seen the new guy? He's so cute. He has these long, pretty eyelashes—" she spread her fingers, waving her hands in front of her eyes.

"Hey, what's about Jake?" I shook my head in disbelief.

"Jake? Jake is mine," she assured me. "No one is better than him for me, human or alien."

"What do you need the deck supervisor for, then?"

She leaned a hip against the cart, looking unimpressed with my inability to grasp her ideas fast enough.

"It's not for me, silly. He'd be for my cousin Becky. Remember her? She's gonna love him," she gushed excitedly. "She's a huge sucker for guys with long eyelashes. He'll love her, too. She's sweet, and funny, and loves to bake. I'm sure they'll get along well."

"You can't pick Ivodians like Christmas gifts for your friends and family," I laughed. "Conqueror isn't a candy shop."

She squinted at me.

"Isn't it? I've seen you drooling from behind the shuttle window when the crew lined up on the dock ever so neatly for your viewing pleasure like in a shop display. And I'm not blaming you. Ivodians are hot dudes, with their hard butts and those muscled arms. What?" she snorted as I rolled my eyes. "I'm engaged, but I'm not blind. I know a great butt when I see one. And there are hundreds of them on this ship."

"I..." I rubbed my forehead. "Okay. Well, that's not what it's about. We're not abducting anyone today."

"No?" She looked genuinely disappointed.

"No," I said firmly.

She folded her arms across her chest, curving her mouth in a displeased frown, but didn't argue anymore.

"Maddy, I need you to help me get to the Central Assembly Room, here on the ship."

"What for?" She narrowed her eyes at me.

"Brigan... I mean Commander Nex is there, at a hearing about, you know... what happened on the weekend."

"Is that his first name? Brigan?"

I nodded.

"Nice," she approved. "Is he in trouble? Are they investigating us taking him?"

I nodded again.

"Are *we* in trouble?" she asked with concern.

"He won't tell on us," I assured her. "But he's facing some serious disciplinary actions because of that. Demotion is among them."

"Shit." She lowered herself on the bed next to me again. "It wasn't his fault, though. He needs to tell them what really happened."

"He won't talk about your involvement at all, don't worry."

She turned to face me.

"I'm not worried about that. I'll go tell them the whole truth myself if it helps."

"It won't help, Maddy. In fact, the truth would only make things worse for him. You see, Ivodians have very peculiar views on the whole abduction thing." I sighed. "It's complicated, with the way their mentality and traditions differ from ours."

"But why do you need to get to that assembly room? Do you think you can do something about what's going on?"

I released a shuddered breath. Dread weighed heavily on my chest.

"I... I need to try, Maddy."

She studied my face for a moment.

"Lori, are you regretting your birthday getaway? Would you rather I hadn't shot him?" she asked with a crestfallen expression.

"What? No." I protested. "I would never regret a single minute spent with Brigan. He is... God, Maddy, he's everything," I groaned. Longing seized my heart with a sweet ache.

A smile curved her lips.

"Does he feel the same way about you?" she asked.

I couldn't help a smile, too. My face warmed up when I thought about all the things Brigan had said to me lately.

"I believe so." I twisted the end of my hair around my finger.

"Well, then it doesn't matter how you guys got together as long as you like each other at the end," she concluded.

"I think it's more than just 'like,' Maddy," I said softly.

She gasped.

"Don't tell me you're in love."

The word "love" rolled like thunder through my brain, yet I couldn't deny the truth.

"It certainly feels that way," I confessed.

"Shit... Oh, Lori. He did turn out to be your soulmate after all!" Maddy grabbed me in a hug. "I'm so happy for you."

I'd be happy, too. Except that I still had to fight for my happiness.

"Can you help me get there, Maddy, please?" I broke our hug and peered at her intently.

"Are you sure you should be moving around? With that thing?" She tipped her chin at the massive cylinder over my leg. "This looks serious."

"I have to."

"But what if you break something again in there?" she worried.

"They'll fix it again." I shrugged. My faith in Ivodian medical skills had grown exponentially after what they'd done so far. Besides, if moving around could cause any serious harm to my leg, the Ivodian who'd brought my lunch wouldn't have offered to take me to the bathroom, especially with this super absorbent diaper-dress I had on. "I need to be at the hearing," I insisted.

"Okay, okay." Maddy rolled the cart closer to the bed, then lowered it until it was the same height. "This is nice." She stroked the black bedding—soft, silky, and luxurious.

"It's pretty," I agreed.

"The whole room is nice." She quickly took in the sitting area by the huge window and the dining space with plush black chairs and small tables that appeared like they could be merged into a large one. "Looks manly but comfy," she concluded. "It would be hard giving this up if they demote your Brigan."

"It'd be much, much harder to give *him* up," I corrected. "If demoted, he'd lose his right to marry, and he'd be sent light years away from me."

She heaved a breath, compassion shining brightly in her dark eyes.

"To marry? It's that serious, huh? You've really fallen for him."

I held her stare, hiding nothing. "I can't lose him, Maddy."

"Well, let's go then." She got hold of the cylinder around my leg. "Does it hurt? Do you feel it?"

I shook my head.

"I feel absolutely nothing. If Brigan hadn't assured me that all is fine, I'd think I had no leg."

She glanced at the cylinder with a new appreciation.

"Sounds like some real cool painkillers." She gently lifted my leg for me while I shifted along the bed, using my arms and hands. I plopped on top of the luggage cart, and Maddy eased the cylinder with my leg down in front of me.

I blew out a breath. The effort proved exhausting.

Maddy shook her head, watching me huff and puff.

"Man, Lori, you should be in bed."

"I'm fine. Maddy, they're going to vote today. I need to be there if I want to have any chance to be heard."

She bit her lip, looking concerned and somewhat doubtful.

"Do you think you can change anything?"

I took a moment to consider my reply. What did I know about this ship or its inhabitants to even attempt to influence their minds in any way? All my knowledge came from when I'd observed them from the cockpit of the shuttle and from what Brigan had told me.

Was it enough?

"I need to try, Maddy. Brigan is my future. I have to fight for us."

She nodded, grabbing the cart handle.

"Well, let's go get them, tiger."

Chapter 17

Lori

The Central Assembly Room was enormous, probably the size of a football field at least. Rows of seats spanned in both directions from the entrance, cascading from top to bottom like sleek, shiny bleachers. Every single seat from the oval floor in the middle to the transparent dome ceiling high above was occupied—rows upon rows of crisp, white uniforms and glistening purple skin of every shade from light cornflower to deep aubergine.

My commander stood at the podium in the middle of the floor, facing three Ivodians who sat in the tall-backed armchairs. These three weren't in uniforms. Instead, they had long, flowing robes on—one was white, the other two in a bright shade of magenta.

Maddy wheeled me in atop the luggage cart.

Everyone turned our way. Curious murmur skittered through the room. The astonishment on their faces told me how ridiculous we...*I* must look, in my loose medical gown, with that huge, cumbersome thing on my leg propped in front of me.

"Lori?" Shock on Brigan's face turned to a frown.

"Who is this woman?" The middle of the three Ivodians in the armchairs enquired in a soft feminine voice. She appeared to be the only woman present.

With a brief bow of his head, Brigan stepped from the podium. "I request a five-minute break, Elder Nex."

Elder Nex.

Brigan's mother.

Great way to meet your boyfriend's parents, Lori.

154

I cringed internally. I had a long record of terrible first impressions with humans, and now, I'd been steadily building one with Ivodians as well.

The nerves got the best of me at the sight of the proceedings—formal and rather intimidating. It seemed like the entire crew of the Conqueror had gathered here, hundreds of them.

Well, I'd come here to speak to all of them, so...

I drew in a bracing breath.

"My name is Lori Soranno. I'm a pilot for Starlight Spacelines. I—I request permission to address the court...um...the hearing," I managed to say loud enough, even if tripping over my words somewhat.

"On what grounds do you demand to speak?" the man in the white robe asked.

He seemed closer in age to Brigan's mom. The man in the deep pink robe appeared older than either of them by at least a decade or so.

"The hearing is almost finished," the older man said. "We have no more speakers on the agenda."

Neon green lights flickered across their face and along the folds of their clothing when they moved. I suddenly realized the three of them weren't actually here. The people in robes were well-executed hologram images.

"On the grounds..." I bit my lip, gathering my thoughts. "Well, I should've been included in the agenda. I'm a witness. The commander spent the weekend with me."

The three brought their heads together, conversing softly between themselves, with not a word reaching me.

I couldn't give them any details about what had happened last weekend without making the things worse for Brigan. I needed to stir this in a different direction entirely.

"Most importantly," I said, even as the three important-looking people no longer appeared to pay me any attention. 'More importantly,

I'm a human woman. I want to give you an insight from the perspective of the abducted bride. Something that I think the Ivodians lack."

The man in the pink robe flicked his wrist dismissively. Brigan's mom straightened in her seat.

"That's not the topic of our discussion today." Elder Nex calmly expressed what they all must be thinking.

I'd never seen an Ivodian woman before. She was much smaller than the men. Her delicate features made her look almost ethereal. Her back straight and her gestures dignified, she held herself with an air of class and elegance. The long pink robe and a tall crystal tiara on her head made for a majestic outfit. Like the men, she had a vertical row of crescents running up the middle of her forehead, but there were no slim streaks of the locators anywhere on her bald head.

I inhaled deeply, bracing for a fight.

"With all due respect, um..." How do I address them? Your Honor, like in court? Your Grace or Your Majesty? They certainly looked like royalty, sitting majestically in those imposing throne-like armchairs. I went with, "...esteemed Elders. The root of so many misunderstandings lies in lack of meaningful conversation. If you let me speak, we may work out a solution."

I darted a glance at Brigan, who was headed my way.

"The hearing is about the conduct of Commander Nex, specifically," the man in the white robe boomed. "It has nothing to do with the current situation with human brides."

"But what if the two are connected?" Of course there must be a connection. I just needed to figure out where and present it in the most favorable light for Brigan.

"Commander, please return to the podium," Elder Nex demanded in a strong voice that clashed with her frail appearance. "You haven't finished your final address yet."

"Commander!" the man in the white robe barked. His commanding voice—so like Brigan's—made me jump to attention.

Brigan didn't seem intimidated, however.

"First and foremost, I need to ensure the safety of Captain Soranno, Councilor Nex," Brigan tossed over his shoulder, not slowing down on his way to me.

"Nex? Councilor Nex?" I whispered when he came closer.

"He's my father," he explained, lowering his voice.

"Both your mom *and* your dad are here?" I flicked my gaze between the stately holograms.

I did not expect the hearing to be a family affair. Though judging by the stern expressions of his parents, Brigan couldn't count much on any leniency or favoritism from them.

"And who's the third one? Your uncle?" I exclaimed.

"No. It's Elder Odu. We're not related," he replied flatly. "I need to get you back to our bedroom. I did not permit anyone to remove you from there." He threw a glance at Maddy, who faltered under his stern stare.

"Well," she chirped. "If you don't need me anymore..." She inched back toward the exit.

I turned to her. "Thank you, Maddy."

"The time I have for this visit is up," she said quickly, keeping an eye on Brigan. "I'll see you later." She wiggled her fingers at both of us.

"*Good luck,*" she mouthed over her shoulder to me before slipping between the two door panels and out of the room.

"I'll take you back." Brigan lifted me in his arms. His tails wrapped around my injured leg, gently sliding it off the luggage cart.

For a moment, I let the world fall away, luxuriating in his closeness. Every minute he'd been away from me, I'd felt like an important part of me was missing. Wrapping my arms around his neck, I melted into his embrace, inhaling his familiar scent.

No one protested about his actions now. The Elders didn't try to stop Brigan from holding me. Ensuring my safety, apparently, was more important than these proceedings. Abducted brides had lots of rights on the Conqueror. I just hoped that speaking their mind was one of those rights, too.

"I can't leave, Brigan," I pleaded softly. "Not until I said what I've come here to say."

"No matter what you do at this point, Lori, you can't change things. There is but one outcome."

He turned toward the exit, and I looked around the room behind him.

The Elders watched us closely. Brigan's parents, I assumed, would be curious about the woman hugging their son. The third Elder also seemed intrigued.

But it was the longing on the faces of the Ivodian warriors when they saw me in Brigan's arms that made me pause.

"Please, let me talk to them," I whispered in Brigan's ear urgently.

"Is that what you really want?" He stopped at the doors. "Even if it's hopeless?"

"I have to try." I nodded.

"You can't lie, Lori," he warned. "They'll know if you do."

I wasn't above bending the truth a little if it meant helping Brigan without harming others. If those at the hearing were capable of telling a lie from the truth, however, lying would only hinder us both.

"I'm not going to lie," I assured him.

He gave me a penetrating look.

"Please trust me." I stroked the side of his face gently. "Whatever I say won't make it any worse than it already is, will it?"

"I can't deny you," he conceded.

Heaving a breath, he turned to face the three officials in the armchairs.

"Captain Soranno will speak here today," he addressed the room in a loud, confident voice. "That is her wish."

He headed back to the podium, carrying me in his arms.

Someone brought a chair for me. Brigan raised it and slid the foot support out from underneath for my leg.

After rolling the chair over to the podium, he lingered, keeping his hand on my shoulder.

"I'll be fine." I smiled up at him.

He swiftly leaned over and caught my mouth in a kiss. I released a gasp of surprise in his mouth, then wound my arms around him tightly.

He broke the kiss as suddenly as he'd started it. And I immediately missed his arms and his lips.

"Don't worry about the Committee," he said softly. "They're here just to ensure the proceedings run smoothly and according to the law. The crew of the Conqueror are the ones who will decide my fate."

I panted a little, catching the breath his kiss had stolen. The warriors stared at us, with unmistakable longing. They wanted what Brigan and I had.

Elder Odu and Brigan's parents seemed less impressed.

His dad's hands gripped the armrests. His mom pressed her lips together tightly, in a similar expression Brigan had when he was displeased or concerned.

"I'll be right here if you need me," Brigan said, stepping aside a couple of paces.

The crew.

His men were the ones I had to convince.

I swept the enormous room with my gaze. Rows upon rows of Ivodian men. All looking at me. What would they be feeling right now? I tried to gauge.

For years, they had risked their lives to earn the right to settle down and start a family. When many of them finally had exercised their right to take a wife, they had to give their women up to save the life of their comrade.

As a human woman, I represented the brides they had lost. Some of the warriors might've built an understanding with their women, some didn't. Most, if not all, would like another chance, I believed.

"Please speak, Captain Soranno," Elder Nex urged.

"But stay on topic," Elder Odu instructed.

On topic.

Right. I shifted closer to the funnel-like device attached to the podium—the speaking device Brigan had been talking about, I assumed.

"The purpose of this hearing is to investigate what happened last weekend." I cast a questioning glance at the three stately figures in front of me, waiting for them to confirm.

They all nodded in agreement.

"I can share with you what happened." I raised my chin, addressing the crew. "I have a cabin...um...a primitive shelter in Northern Ontario, which is...well, in the Northern Hemisphere of our planet. It belonged to my grandfather, and I love going there, every chance I get. You see, it's a special place for me. A happy place..."

It wasn't easy to share my deepest emotions with hundreds of aliens who knew nothing about me, but I kept going.

"It has no modern amenities. No electricity or running water. No phone or Internet access. Away from civilization, that place allows a person to be themselves. That's one of the reasons why I love it so much."

Elder Odu rubbed a side of his creased forehead.

"How does it relate to the commander?" he asked, looking tired.

"It does," I assured him, bobbing my head. "Last weekend, Commander Nex shared my cabin with me, giving me a chance to get to know him. I've learned what kind of a man he truly is, and I fell in love with that man."

A rumble rolled over the rows, reaching up to the stars beyond the glass ceiling.

Brigan snapped his gaze to mine. His chest rose and fell rapidly. There was so much in his violet eyes—shock, excitement, and endless tenderness—it made my heart ache.

I smiled just for him. His tails twitched, one of them slinking my way. It wound around my left wrist, and I wrapped my fingers around its tip, the closest I could get to holding Brigan's hand at the moment. Emotions misted my eyes, but I blinked the tears away, needing to focus.

I'd just started. I needed to see this through.

"If he were to abduct me, now," I continued, turning back to the room. "I'd go with him willingly."

Another wave of noise rolled over the crowd. The clear note of approval in it gave me hope.

Other than Brigan, I'd hardly spoken to Ivodians. I didn't know them. But I'd watched them carefully before. Each flight to the Conqueror, I'd seen them saying goodbye to the women they had chosen. And I'd guessed correctly—Ivodians didn't just want a woman in their bed, they wanted her love and affection, too.

"What did it for you? What made you fall in love with my son?" Elder Nex tilted her head, regarding me with new interest. "Because being alone with their husbands didn't prove enough for the Conqueror's brides. Many spent much more time than two days with their men, and still there was no sign of affection on their part."

"Hhm," Brigan's dad rubbed his chin. "It's been determined that human women generally don't find our men attractive enough."

"Who determined that?" I scoffed, making a face.

"A panel of highly qualified specialists," Elder Odu replied, looking highly unimpressed with my reaction. "If compared side by side, an average Ivodian man significantly differs from an average human male in appearance. Psychologically, women tend to find attractive more familiar features."

"The representatives of the Coalition of Earth's Governments also agree with our findings," Elder Nex chimed in.

"Well," I cleared my throat. "Maybe you should've asked our women directly. Take it from me, these guys are hot." I swept the room with my right arm. My left had been firmly claimed by Brigan's tail.

"Hot?" Brigan's dad asked, squinting at me.

I waved my hand in the air, explaining, "By hot, I mean extremely attractive." I then raised my voice, addressing the crew in the seats all around us. "As a human woman I swear, you are a handsome bunch."

An uneasy murmur met my words. I couldn't believe I had to convince these strong, confident men that they're likable.

"Your statements contradict the numerous reports we got from the warriors who had the misfortune to acquire human brides," Elder Odu informed me.

"Misfortune?" I echoed, suddenly feeling offended for all womankind.

"We expected a resistance from human men to our actions," he continued, ignoring my tone. "Every race we know, be it the Ravils or the Voranians, would object to us taking their women—it's insulting to men's honor. We were prepared to deal with that. But it's the strong disdain of the women that came as a shock to us."

He dropped his shoulders in obvious disappointment.

"Instead of happiness and gratitude, many of the warriors encountered misery and hostility from their human brides." A hologram screen lit up in front of Elder Odu, and he squinted, reading from the list displayed on it. "According to the reports, the warriors have been called 'ugly' and 'disgusting' by their brides. The Ivodians' tails were compared to *snakes*—an animal generally thought of as repulsive on Earth and on many other planets. Many of the crew reported being referred to by the word that means 'anal opening,' which is considered offensive in every known culture."

Tilting his head, he leveled me a stare, daring me to disagree.

"Right..." I heaved a sigh, mumbling, "I can see how that would happen."

"So, you agree that either physical or emotional attraction is not commonly possible between our species? In fact, humans generally experience severe repulsion toward Ivodians."

I rolled back my shoulders, gripping Brigan's tail tighter.

"I believe the lack of attraction is not the issue here, Elder Odu," I said. "I'm sorry, but humans just generally don't appreciate being kidnapped."

All three of them winced at my last word as if I'd just fed them a bucket of cranberries without sugar.

"Bridal abduction is not *kidnapping*," Elder Nex protested fiercely. "It's not done to harm or extort. On the contrary, women are treated with respect and taken care of, in every way."

"Well, that was not communicated to the women, was it?" I retorted.

"Of course it was," she bristled. "The protocol demands that every warrior clearly informs the woman about her status as a bride the moment she sets her foot in the shuttle. All warriors confirmed they had repeated it frequently throughout the duration of their bride's stay on the Conqueror."

I glanced at Brigan, and he returned my knowing look. Clearly, he remembered how mistrustful he'd been of me those first few hours of him being "abducted" by me, no matter how often I'd said I meant no harm and wasn't a spy.

"Please, look at it from the perspective of a woman, a *human* woman." I turned to the rest of the room. "Here, on Earth, we don't sit around waiting for men to come and claim us. We don't plan on being abducted by anyone. We plan our own future. Most of us have jobs or attend school. We have our friends and family—"

"Marriage to an Ivodian doesn't sever the bride's ties with her family," Elder Odu interrupted. "Family is important on Ivodi, the bride's family included. All abducted women were made aware of that."

I decided not to clarify in what way they were "made aware." Obviously, the communication had been broken between the warriors and their brides, one way or another.

"The fact remains," I continued. "The women were grabbed off the streets without knowing what was happening. Just think about it. Look at all of this through the eyes of a human woman, who's used to walking on the streets by herself." I remembered what Brigan had told me about the life of women on Ivodi and added, "Women in most places on Earth don't need to be accompanied by a male relative. They feel fairly safe walking on their own. Suddenly, a flying saucer comes out of nowhere—"

"A saucer?" Councilor Nex lifted an eyebrow ridge, looking very much like Brigan when he was confused.

"Sorry, I meant the Ivodian shuttle, an aircraft that humans hadn't seen before." There was no need to get into the explanation of the word "saucer," even if that was exactly what the shuttles of the Conqueror looked like—silver flying saucers. "Then, a stranger grabs her. He's large and intimidating. Not ugly." I lifted a finger in the air to emphasize the point. "Not ugly, but utterly unfamiliar. He speaks a language the woman can't understand—"

"The brides had translators implanted almost immediately," Elder Odu interrupted again.

Brigan's parents both kept silent. His dad held his chin in his hand, his arm propped into the chair's armrest, a frown of concentration on his weathered face. With a slight tilt of her head, Brigan's mom appeared to be listening with rapt attention.

"*Almost* immediately," I repeated slowly, for added emphasis. "For a period of time, no matter how short, the woman was left in a complete terror of not knowing what's going on and whether she'll live or die."

"A bride's life is *never* in danger!" Brigan's dad bellowed indignantly.

My heart leaped, and I swallowed a gasp. The men in this family possessed the most intimidating voices.

Coils of Brigan's tail slid up and down my wrist, soothing me.

"But the human brides didn't know that their lives weren't threatened," I argued, standing my ground. "At the moment of the abduction, they were scared, shocked, and confused. That is not a good start to a relationship. No wonder that many of them never recovered from that and never warmed up to their abductors."

Silence descended on the room. It reigned over the crowd long after the echo of my words dissolved under the dome ceiling.

Elder Odu stirred first.

"We have done our research," he said. "The welcoming speeches were designed to reflect local customs of each bride."

They very well might have. Ivodians appeared to have done some due diligence. It just didn't prove enough.

"The damage was done before the women heard even a word of your welcoming speeches," I pointed out. "But there is more."

"More?" Elder Nex furrowed her delicate eyebrow ridges.

I nodded.

"Many of those abducted weren't even free to commit. They weren't single. They already had men they cared about in their lives."

Elder Odu shook his head vehemently.

"Impossible. We've looked into it. Human men claim a woman by gifting her a ring of commitment, which she then wears on a certain finger, either on her right or left hand depending on the region she comes from. The instructions were not to abduct women with rings on those fingers."

"Oh, boy." I sucked in a breath, getting ready to explain as best as I could. "A lot happens between a couple before they put a ring on it.

Here on Earth, we have what we call 'dating.' We take time choosing our partners."

"That's not how it's supposed to be," Elder Odu scoffed. "A man knows his chosen one the moment he first lays his eyes on her."

Obviously the one thing Ivodian and human men had in common was stubbornness.

"How do you *date?*" The question came from one of the crew to my right.

An Ivodian warrior rose from his seat. His tails fanned behind him, lashing impatiently. I wondered if the tails were the reason the higher officials of Ivodi wore robes—to conceal the appendages that could so easily betray their emotions.

"How do you choose?" the man asked.

Light muttering of voices ran between the rows of seating. The men seemed curious. Intrigued.

"'Dating' means spending time together to learn more about the other person before committing your life to them. Like Commander Nex did when he joined me on my getaway to my grandpa's cabin. He gave me the chance to get to know him." I couldn't help a glance at my man.

He met my gaze, a ghost of a smile playing on his lips. His tail in my hand twitched, the coils around my wrist sliding up and down my arm in a caress.

Another Ivodian raised his tails in the air, demanding to speak.

"Do all women on Earth have a primitive shelter where they like to get away?" he asked.

"Um... No." I shook my head, hiding a smile. "I doubt many do. Roughing it in the wilderness is not for everyone."

"How do we let them get to know us, then?" Another man asked.

The room grew quiet, everyone waiting for my answer. This was encouraging. Finally, someone was really listening to me. And those were the most important people here—the crew.

"You don't have to travel far away to get to know each other. Most people date by having a meal together in a restaurant nearby or watching a movie at home. Even going for a walk together would work. You just need a place where you can talk without too many distractions and enough time to have a meaningful interaction. The most important part is that the woman feels safe. She needs to know she can leave anytime, that she's free."

The brow ridges of the man who'd asked the question rose high. He seemed genuinely confused.

"How is she free if she's my bride?" He blinked. "She can't leave. She's mine."

"Well, that's the thing," I said slowly. "She's not your bride until she agrees to be."

The silence that followed was only interrupted by people shifting in their seats and by feet shuffling.

Traditions didn't change overnight, as Brigan had said to me once. However, I felt I could possibly nudge this toward an acceptable solution. These men wanted to learn. Fundamentally, I believed, they wished to do the right thing. I just needed to explain to them *how*.

"If I may..." I lifted my hand in the air, calling to their attention. "I have a suggestion that may help you get a bride who is willing and loving. One you won't need to lock in your bedroom because she'll be happy to stay there with you. One who won't call you nasty names, either because she won't be scared or angry."

A roar of approval from the crew mixed with doubtful grunts. I needed to build on whatever support I'd gained so far.

"What's better than having a wife who loves you for who you are?" I asked, peering into the crowd.

Someone yelled from his seat suddenly, "Zenya loves me! I'm not leaving Earth without getting her back."

I wondered if Zenya had been one of the women who sobbed quietly when leaving the Conqueror.

"The moment Urrex is released, I'm abducting my bride again!" someone else shouted.

"We're not leaving without what we've come here for!" another one yelled.

Were those cries of a broken heart? Bruised ego?

Or a real threat?

I glanced at Brigan. His hard expression told me everything he hadn't said before. Ivodians weren't giving up on the abductions. The Coalition might've stopped them for now, but only temporarily. They would abduct again, with or without Earth's consent.

If that happened, the conflict was inevitable.

Dread seized my throat. Weapons would be fired. People might die. Unless both parties came to an agreement, somehow.

Our officials could be just as stubborn as Ivodians. But maybe I could manage to get at least one side willing to negotiate.

"I propose Ivodians give dating a try," I said loud enough to hopefully be heard in every part of the room without a chance for misunderstanding.

A murmur of questions rolled through the crowd, none distinct enough for me to answer.

Brigan's mom rested her chin upon her hand.

"How would you suggest we do it, Captain Soranno?" she enquired.

All I had was that half-baked plan I'd come up with during the conversation with Brigan while hiking through the woods. Thinking about it now, I figured it was a good start.

"Brigan… I mean Commander Nex and I have discussed it during our time together," I started. "I believe many human women would love to have an Ivodian husband—"

A roar of disbelief from the crowd drowned out the rest of my words.

"Not true!" someone yelled over the noise.

"They hate us!" another man shouted.

I squinted against the ray of soft light directed at me and recognized the first engineer as the one who yelled last. He obviously was still bitter about Felicity's rejection. Yet they still were going to abduct more women, knowing they might be hated by them again.

"It doesn't need to be a struggle," I said confidently. "It can be so much better, for everyone. Look at me. I'm from Earth. Brigan is from Ivodi. And I want no one else but him."

His tail around my wrist tightened. All this time, Brigan had been quietly standing at my side. I felt his support every moment while being in the spotlight. His presence gave me strength.

"You may be an exception." Elder Odu shook his bald, wrinkly head.

I made an effort not to glare at him.

"Well, let the women decide." I then spoke to the crew again, "Please, allow our women to apply to be your brides, by choice. Give them a chance to get to know you first. Go on dates, spend some time together. When a woman really likes you, she'd come with you to the Conqueror willingly. I promise you that."

"Do you have an idea on how the *dating* could be achieved?" Elder Nex asked.

"Will you be willing to consult on this project, provided it's approved, of course?" Councilor Nex inquired next.

I inclined my head. "I'd be happy to help in any way I can."

The project would be essentially setting up an alien dating agency, which could be fun if done right.

Earth already had a marriage agreement with Voranians. Except that it had some major flaws, in my opinion. To my knowledge, our women didn't have enough control over which Voranian they would get matched with.

If I had a chance to do it from scratch, I would definitely try to avoid making the same mistake Earth had made with Voranians. Women needed to have more control over their future.

The Ivodians had messed it up with our women once already. They would need all the help they could get to do it properly the next time.

"I don't see harm in trying a new approach," Elder Nex said to her husband. "Since the old one proved disastrous for us on this planet."

With a look full of admiration, Brigan closed the distance between us. His arms and tails wound around me. Pleasure rippled through me, warming my chest. Was it true? Were the things really looking up? Did I manage to help him by speaking up?

It wasn't over yet, but the mood in the room seemed to have lifted. Excitement rippled between the rows of seating. The Ivodians got hope again.

I smiled so wide, my face hurt.

Brigan's comm beeped.

"Commander, the Coalition is demanding the return of Captain Soranno to Earth with today's shuttle," a male voice conveyed impassionedly.

My heart dropped.

Chapter 18

Lori

"The captain is staying here," Brigan bit off into the comm device. His tails wound tightly around my middle, as if someone was about to physically wrench me away from him.

The device went silent. I clutched Brigan's hand in mine.

"That's a part of your agreement with the Coalition," I reminded him softly. The noise of the Ivodians discussing my proposal muffled my words so only Brigan could hear me. "If I don't go, they'll…"

"They're not getting you." He held me to him tightly, with the desperation of a man about to lose his most treasured possession.

"All abducted women have to be returned before they release your Second-in-Command," I said. "The Coalition sees me as one of the abductees as well." I couldn't tell the Coalition the truth without risking hurting Brigan's standing with his crew.

"You don't understand. I can't let you leave." He kneeled in front of my chair, his arms around me. "You're mine, Lori. I'd fight all the worlds for you."

I placed my hands on his shoulders. Being near him was the only place I wanted to be.

The damn comm beeped again.

"The Coalition Rep is requesting to speak with you, Commander," the male on the other end of the line said with obvious disdain for the rep in his voice.

"No—" Brigan started, but I cupped his face, afraid he might truly start a war over me.

"This may be only temporary," I said quietly.

He shook his head.

"We'll fight, Brigan. I'll fight with you. But we'll have to use a diplomatic approach," I implored. "Otherwise, we'll risk ruining everything we've achieved so far."

"Commander," Councilor Nex said loudly. "Are the crew ready for the vote?"

"What vote are you talking about?" I looked up, alarmed.

Were they voting? Already?

"This hearing is to investigate the commander's absence from the ship and to assess the crew's trust in their leader," Elder Nex summed up.

Elder Odu added, "If the crew are satisfied with the findings of the investigation, they'll vote on whether they trust the commander to continue leading them and helm the Conqueror."

I twisted in my seat, taking in as many of the warriors' faces as I could. Brigan's—and my—fate was in their hands.

"Commander Nex is a true leader," I said loudly, rushing to reinforce my message. "By spending the weekend with me, he laid the groundwork for you. What he did can be the beginning of a much stronger relationship between Ivodi and Earth. A relationship of mutual respect and open communication between our planets and between you and your future brides—"

The comm beeped again. That thing just wouldn't quit.

"What should I say to the rep?" the male voice enquired.

Brigan got to his feet and lifted me from my seat.

"Any more witnesses, Commander?" Elder Odu tried to stop us. "Or shall we proceed with the vote?"

"Let them vote." Brigan headed for the exit with me in his arms.

"Wait!" I panicked. "Don't you want to say something to them? Like give a speech or something? Tell them you trust them to support you?"

"I trust them," he said simply. "The vote is about *them* trusting *me*. I've said everything I had to say before you showed up." His lips twitched in a smile. "Before you rolled in on the luggage cart like a woman on a mission."

I'd smile at that, too, if I wasn't so anxious and stressed.

"But—" I gripped his shoulders, fervently scanning the faces of the crew behind him. As if I could influence their decision with just a gaze, no matter how desperate and imploring.

Brigan pressed me to his chest.

"I'm afraid I'm losing something far more precious to me than my position." He carried me out of the Assembly Room and down a wide, brightly lit corridor. "Get the rep on the line," he barked into the comm.

I held my breath, scared to move for the few seconds it took them to connect.

"Commander Nex?" another male voice spoke. "My name is Jason Grey, I'm calling on behalf of the Coalition of the Earth's Governments. It's been confirmed you have Ms. Lori Soranno—"

"*Captain* Soranno," Brigan corrected briskly.

I just shrugged. My civil aviation rank normally wasn't used outside of the craft I flew. The Ivodians, however, seemed to place a much higher importance on ranks and titles than they did on given names.

"She is not leaving," Brigan said firmly, not letting the rep even voice his request.

"Allow me to remind you that the condition of our agreement—"

"I said, Captain Soranno is not going anywhere."

"Mister Grey," I squeezed a word in. Obviously, this conversation was headed for a standstill, with two male egos battling each other like mountain goats. "I would like to request a meeting with someone from the Coalition, please."

"Ms. Soranno, rest assured that like the other women released from the Conqueror, you will be provided with every support you need."

"Thank you, but I would like to discuss the situation with someone as soon as possible."

"We have an excellent team of counselors—"

"That's not what I mean." My patience was growing thin. Like Brigan, I felt strongly about our impending separation. Unlike him, I preferred a peaceful resolution instead of confrontation, but the rep was really trying my patience. "If I leave, I want to talk to someone about my return to the Conqueror."

"You want to return to the ship." It came as a statement, not a question. The rep didn't sound particularly surprised. I couldn't be the only one who wished to come back.

"Yes. In fact, I'd prefer to remain here now." I had to say that on the record.

"I'm afraid we can't allow for you to stay," the rep said flatly. "Sorry, Ms. Soranno, but considering the circumstances, your judgement may currently be impaired. You may not be in the best position to see what's best for you."

I huffed a laugh in disbelief.

"I'm a competent adult of sound mind. I am capable of making my own decisions," I protested.

"Not in this situation," he argued. "It's been decided that all abducted women have to be removed from the Conqueror. It's necessary for them to form independent judgements after a period spent away from their captors."

"You just can't believe that our women can have genuine feelings for aliens," I scoffed.

"Ma'am, given the circumstances of how the women happened to be on the Conqueror in the first place, the decision of the Coalition to take them away is reasonable and warranted."

Maybe it held true for the abducted women—I wasn't a specialist in mental health. Despite my own words about a diplomatic approach,

I just couldn't bring myself to part from Brigan. I wrapped my arms tighter around his neck.

"Your presence on that ship violates the agreement we have with Commander Nex," the rep continued. "If you don't come to Earth with today's shuttle, you will jeopardize the peace between our planets."

There was more than that. The life of Officer Urrex was still on the line. As long as I remained on the Conqueror, the Coalition wouldn't release him.

Yet tearing myself from Brigan seemed impossible. Painfully hard.

"Can I take the last flight? Tomorrow?" I grasped at the straws.

"Tomorrow's shuttle is full. There is no room for you. Your presence on the Conqueror is unexpected. We didn't plan for an extra passenger. The last flight was filled fast. You must understand we're being lenient by giving Commander Nex a chance to return you peacefully and of his own accord."

Brigan huffed. His chest rose with a sharp breath. Whatever he was going to say, I sensed it would not help the situation. Judging by his stormy expression, it all could get much worse very quickly.

"Fine. I'll be there," I blurted out into the comm, then placed my hand over the device, blocking all sounds.

Just in time it seemed, as Brigan roared, "By the Serpent of Ahell! They can't have you!"

He lashed with a tail against the wall, and a panel slid aside, revealing his bedroom.

I hadn't even realized we'd made it here already.

His tails wound so tightly around me, I could barely move a muscle. I pressed the side of my face to his.

"Listen," I whispered in his ear. "What if we can fix this? All of it? For everyone, not just you and me?" I wanted to believe we could, so badly. "But not like this. For now, you'll have to give me up."

He jerked his head in protest, but I held on to his shoulders tightly and kept on speaking.

"They're only demanding from you what your men have already done. If the crew can do it, so can their leader."

"The crew didn't have to give up *you*." He sounded bitter and outright heartbroken. My heart was breaking for both of us, too.

"I believe some of them cared about their women just as strongly, Brigan."

"They will get them back."

"So will you," I assured him softly. "I'm not going far, and I'm not leaving for good. I told you I'm yours, no matter what. I'll come back. But I need to do as the Coalition wants, for now. Remember, they have one of your men. We can't risk his life."

I hoped so badly it wouldn't come down to a bloodshed. Would the Coalition really go so far as to murder an Ivodian over this? I hoped not, but what did I know about high politics? They had already gone so far as to kidnap and threaten Brigan's Second-in-Command. I could only hope there were some reasonable people in the Coalition that would agree to listen and to allow me to return to Brigan.

Because if not...

Well, if I wasn't here, who would hold him back from starting a war?

Holding me tightly, his back to the wall, he slid down to sit on the floor.

"I will lock the doors. Send the shuttle back. Annihilate anyone who dares approach you," he gritted through his teeth.

It was no longer his reason speaking but desperation. He sounded like a man gone mad. Dread chilled me. I wasn't afraid for myself but for the rest of the planet. The weapons on the Conqueror were dangerous enough to cause serious damage and kill a lot of people.

And it would be all because of me.

"Brigan, please." I took his face between my hands, forcing him to meet my eyes. My fingers trailed along the short rows of the toothpick-like locator implants on each side of his head—five on the left, only four on the right, now. "The moment I get back to Earth, I'll demand a meeting with the Coalition rep. Maybe we can change this? But we'll have to work from both sides—you from here, and me from back home."

He shut his eyes. I racked my brain on how to get through to him. How could I cheer him up, at least for a little bit?

I nuzzled the side of his face and whispered into his ear, "Just make sure you have your translator fixed. We don't want any naughty misunderstandings with the Coalition reps."

It worked for a moment—he huffed a laugh and opened his eyes. As he saw my smile, however, his expression turned pained again. He hugged me tighter and shook his head.

"If you leave... I'll have no control over what's done to you. I can't protect you. What if something happens? What if I never see you again?" he croaked, his voice raw.

My heart ached. I struggled to hold it together myself.

"Brigan, I promise, I'll come back to you. Here with you is the only place I want to be."

He gazed into my eyes intently.

"I can't deny you anything, Lori, even if you want to leave. But you are my life. I can't be without you. I can't breathe without you. If they try to keep you away from me, no agreement will hold me back." A grave, threatening note slipped into his voice. A threat for anyone who would dare keep me away from him. "Do you understand? I will not leave this planet without you. No matter what it'll take to get you back."

I didn't want to imagine the devastation he could cause.

"I will come back, Brigan," I promised again. And I'd better keep that promise, for the sake of everyone on Earth.

He groaned, tossing his head back.

"How am I supposed to let you go?" he bellowed, his deep voice reverberating through the spacious room. "I'd rather tear off a limb!"

I blinked tears out of my eyes, needing to be strong for both of us.

"This is only temporary, Brigan. I'll be back soon. A week, maybe two?"

I had no idea how long it would take for the Coalition to cooperate, if ever. Anything longer than two weeks, however, seemed like an eternity. I didn't even want to consider that.

Still, he held me, not moving from our spot on the floor.

"Your leg." A few of his tails slid gently along the cumbersome but lightweight cylinder protecting my healing leg.

"It'll be fine, thanks to you." I stroked the side of his face. "The surgery is finished. It just needs to heal now. I'll stay at home and rest. I can communicate with the Coalition remotely, but I need to be on Earth for them to calm down and listen rationally. You can write to me. They'll have to allow that at least."

He buried his face in the side of my neck, breathing me in.

I stroked his head gently, fighting back tears ready to burst free.

"I won't just have to let you go," he groaned. "I'll need to carry you all the way back to that fucking shuttle, place you in the seat with my own hands, then watch them take you away from me."

"You don't have to do all that, Brigan. Do you have a wheelchair around here?" I swallowed the lump in my throat, faking a lighter tone. "Or I could just take the luggage cart again?"

He didn't laugh at my joke attempt.

"You don't need a wheelchair, not as long as you're with me." He got to his feet, effortlessly taking me with him.

The moment he stepped out of the room, a hard, severe expression firmly settled over his face. Any trace of vulnerability I might've glimpsed when we were alone was gone. Brigan was the commander, through and through, whether he managed to keep that title today or not.

He carried me all the way into the shuttle, placed me in the seat, and even buckled me in. Leaning closer, he kissed me. It was a long, deep kiss that ended way too soon.

"Remember, you're my life, Lori," he said softly, cupping my face.

I bit my lip, holding my tears back with everything I had.

He'd claimed me, pledged his life and his loyalty to me. He'd committed to me without doubt or reservations after but one weekend together. That required courage no other man I knew possessed.

And somehow, in that short time, he'd managed to become my everything.

Chapter 19

Lori

"Hello, Lori Soranno?" a female voice on my phone enquired. "It's Zenya. Zenya Petrenko. We were on the shuttle together yesterday."

I remembered the young blonde woman with sad, swollen eyes. She'd sat across the aisle from me and introduced herself before we'd disembarked. Other than her name, she hadn't said much.

"Sorry, I had to do some snooping to get your number..." she said with a nervous giggle.

For a moment, I considered hanging up. It'd been twenty-four hours since I'd left the Conqueror—one long day and a restless night without a word from Brigan. He hadn't written, and I was too anxious to speak to anyone else.

"I—I saw you kissing the commander of the Ivodian ship," Zenya continued, hesitantly. "And I wondered if maybe...I could talk to you."

"Talk about what?"

"Well..." She didn't appear prepared for this conversation, stumbling over words and taking long pauses. "You see... I know other girls were happy to go home, so I didn't think they'd understand. But you..." Her voice trailed off, but I believed I understood her.

"You wanted to speak to someone who may be willing to return to the Conqueror. Is that it?" I asked carefully, no longer wishing to end this call.

"Yes," she exhaled with obvious relief. "I wonder if you're planning to go back."

Planning.

If only it was up to me. So far, I've had one brief meeting with a Coalition rep right after getting off the shuttle last night. He listened when I told him my visit to the Conqueror was voluntary and that I wished to return. However, he had nothing encouraging to say in reply.

Shortly after I'd come to my condo, though, another rep from the Coalition called to inform me of a meeting being scheduled for tomorrow morning. This one was with a group of people from several government agencies. I wasn't sure whether it happened in response to my request or if the Ivodians had applied some pressure from their end. It could be both, of course.

"Yes," I replied to Zenya's question honestly. "I would like to return to the Conqueror."

"Oh, thank God," she breathed out. "I'm so glad I called. The way the commander and you kissed, I knew it couldn't be the end for the two of you."

I bit my lip, trying not to think about how amazing Brigan's mouth felt against my lips, lest I fall apart right now while on the phone with her.

"I have to get back to Naitas, too," Zenya said softly, her voice full of hope.

"Naitas? Is he the one who abducted you?"

"Yes."

I remembered the Ivodian who had claimed at the hearing that his Zenya loved him. There could be more than one Zenya abducted, of course, but somehow I knew it was the same man and that this was his Zenya.

"When he snatched me from that bridge, I was at the end of my rope," Zenya continued hurriedly. "That night, I left a...um...a very bad situation at home, and I really had no place to go. I honestly don't know if I would've walked off that bridge or just..."

Her voice trailed off again, and my heart swelled with compassion.

"Zenya, where are you now?"

"In a women's shelter. It's not bad. Really. The Coalition made sure I have everything I need. I get counselling, but..." she drew in a breath. "I just miss him so much, Lori." Her voice shook, and my eyes misted with empathy.

I missed Brigan, too. So much, I cried myself to sleep last night.

"What does your therapist say?" I asked carefully.

"I just had one session so far. This morning. It was good. Really, it was very good to talk to someone. But Naitas was the first one who ever listened. He was the one who got me to open up, for the first time. He's so patient, you know. Nothing like my parents or my ex..."

Her voice broke off again, and I waited for a few moments until she composed herself.

"The therapist says it's too early to know if my feelings for Naitas are real. They want me to wait, to take my time, to see if I could build a life for myself on my own first, but... I'm afraid if I wait, the Conqueror will leave. Then, it will be too late."

"You want to be with Naitas?"

"There is no other place I'd rather be." Her voice lifted. "He's the only man I want."

"I have a meeting with people from the Coalition tomorrow morning. You can join me. I'm hoping to work out a way for those who want to return to the Conqueror to reunite with their Ivodians."

"Oh, do you really think it's possible?"

"I hope so." Because otherwise there would be war. I didn't doubt that. And it wouldn't be just Brigan's doing. Men like Naitas must be champing at the bit to get their women back, too. "Would you like to join me for the meeting, Zenya?"

"Yes," she eagerly agreed.

"Great. I'll meet you at ten on the stairs in front of City Hall then. That's where the delegation from the Coalition is holding these meetings. Oh, and Zenya, if you ever decide to leave the shelter, you can stay at my place. It's just a condo, not overly big. But it has two bedrooms. One of them can be yours for as long as you need it."

I hadn't gotten a word from Brigan yet. I had no idea what was happening on the Conqueror. For all I knew, he could have been stripped of his position. Someone else could be the ship's commander, now. Someone who had no interest in human brides and the trouble they presented.

But I hoped there were more Ivodians like Zenya's Naitas out there. That they would want to find a solution to this situation, along with us. No matter what.

THAT NIGHT, I FINALLY got a message from Brigan. It came heavily censored, twice forwarded, but it came, nevertheless. My heart skipped a beat when I realized it was from him. He'd kept it civil and rather cold. If he'd used any tender words, they had been edited out.

He asked me how I was doing, then added a few more general sentences, and signed it as Commander Nex, not Brigan.

I kept staring at the screen of my laptop, reading and re-reading his words and refusing to believe that was all he had to say to me after twenty-four hours of silence.

The more I studied the message, however, the clearer its meaning became. There was more to it than could be seen at first glance.

The time stamp of the original message was shortly before the shuttle's landing yesterday. He literally wrote and sent it before I'd even arrived back on Earth.

All communication from the Conqueror had to go through the Coalition's office. So, the message must've been sitting in someone's inbox, then bounced from one official to another, until it finally reached me.

Since the vote started while I was still on the Conqueror, by signing it as *"Commander Nex"* right after, Brigan was telling me that the crew had voted in his favor. Brigan was still the commander of the Conqueror. I silently thanked whatever higher power was out there. He'd managed to keep the respect of his people.

A couple of sentences at the very end puzzled me the longest.

"You know I treasure my life more than anything," he wrote. *"I'll do everything to keep it."*

This made no sense. Why would he say it? Was his life being threatened in any way on the Conqueror? But why?

Then it dawned on me. Brigan called *me* his life. He must have known that his message would go through censorship by the Coalition in addition to possibly being seen by the Conqueror's Security Team, so he encrypted it.

What he truly meant was, *"I treasure you more than anything. I'll do everything to keep you.*

My heart swelled with longing. Tears gathered in my eyes again.

"I'll do everything to come back to you, Brigan," I whispered, splaying my hand on the screen over his words. "I swear, I'll fight them."

So, I did.

I went to the meeting with the Coalition, armed with a long list of arguments. Zenya came with me and proved incredibly supportive.

When that meeting ended with the statement *"Ivodians are not good for our women"* from the Coalition, I started tracking down the released women.

I talked to them one-on-one, as many as I could get to agree to speak with me, regardless of whether they wanted to return to the Conqueror or not. I listened to their experiences of staying on the ship and interacting with their abductors.

Some of the women wished nothing to do with the Ivodians. But quite a few expressed an interest in possibly having a date with the warrior who'd taken then released them. And some of the previously abducted "brides" wished to return to the Conqueror as soon as possible.

Most importantly, none of the abducted women—not even those who were still angry about being taken—reported any abuse on the part of their captors, beyond the forced confinement on the ship.

Zenya moved in with me that week. Despite getting a job in a clothing store, she found the time to attend all Coalition meetings with me.

At first, I was getting around in a wheelchair. In just a week, however, the cumbersome cylinder was removed. I moved on to a pair of crutches, and a week later, to just a walking stick.

"If there was a reason for me to demand that Ivodians would stick around longer," my doctor said, twisting the discarded cylinder in her hands. "It would be this. I'd love for them to share their healing technique with us."

Because of that *technique*, the grave injury that would've normally taken weeks if not months to heal, hardly bothered me after just two weeks. I still limped a little and used a walking stick on the advice of my doctor, but I could move independently.

Brigan wrote to me regularly, once a day as per the schedule established by the Coalition. Despite their rigorous censorship, he always managed to slip in a word or two that conveyed how he truly felt. I sensed the tenderness in his words, no matter how heavily redacted. His words gave me hope.

Every now and then, he'd join remotely our meetings with the Coalition. I wished I could at least see his hologram, but only his voice over the speaker device in the middle of the table was allowed.

However, even just hearing his voice was a treat. I would resist the urge to close my eyes and lose myself in that deep, rich sound, remembering the soft, velvety note it took when he'd spoken to me and me alone.

"Does anyone have anything to add?" Jason Grey asked the meeting room once, after Brigan had finished speaking about the program I'd outlined to him back while we'd hiked through the woods up North. The Ivodians had been developing my idea further. And by now, it seemed like a solid plan.

"Yes." I raised my hand. I had plenty to say about the program that had become dear to my heart, but I also simply wanted for Brigan to hear my voice, too.

"Ms. Soranno." Jason nodded, granting me permission to speak.

The silence in the communication device appeared to charge with tension when Jason had said my name. I couldn't see him, but I knew Brigan was listening intently.

"It's time to narrow down the timelines," I said, softly, feeling like I was talking to Brigan alone. "We've been waiting patiently, and we deserve to know when the wait is over."

"That could be discussed next." Another rep asserted, twisting the pen of his tablet between his fingers.

"Today," Brigan's voice boomed from the device. "We will discuss it right now."

My breath hitched at the force in his words. His presence seemed to fill the entire room, despite him not even being physically here.

"Commander—" one of the reps tried to protest.

"We've been talking about this for weeks," Brigan cut him off. "All your questions have been answered, many times over. It's time to move ahead."

Another rep waved at Zenya and me, along with the three other women who'd come to the meeting with us.

"Your presence is no longer necessary," he said quickly, gesturing for us to leave the room. "Thank you for your input."

I remained seated.

"I'm not leaving unless I'm updated on what has been decided the moment a decision is reached."

He made a face but conceded, "We'll call all of you as soon as we know."

Outside of City Hall, the five of us lingered on the wide stairs. The three other women then all said their goodbyes and left, one by one.

Zenya and I had hotdogs from a food cart for lunch in the nearby parkette.

"Hopefully something will be decided today," I said as we were sitting on the bench together.

"Oh, I hope so." Zenya heaved a sigh, feeding crumbs of her hotdog bun to a pigeon trotting on the paving stones nearby. "It's been nerve-racking. I don't know what I'd do if I didn't have you, Lori." She glanced at me.

During the past two weeks and a bit, Zenya had visibly changed. We all were stressed, but she no longer looked lost. She appeared much calmer, despite the uncertainties we'd been dealing with. Her confidence had greatly improved, too.

"I'm so happy we've met, Zenya," I said, feeling genuinely glad about having her with me through all of this.

"Me too." She leaned closer, giving me a big hug. "Well, I'd better get to work. My shift is starting soon." She got up, shaking the crumbs off her skirt to the utter delight of the pigeon. "Are you okay getting home on your own? Are you taking an Uber?"

I shook my head.

"I'll take the subway. It'd probably be faster, anyway. The station is right there." I waved at the street behind the parkette.

She heaved another sigh.

"Well, I'll see you tonight. Hopefully, we hear something soon."

I nodded. "Hopefully."

For as long as the Conqueror remained in orbit, there was hope. I resisted the urge to search the sky for its light. It was barely past noon. I wouldn't be able to see a thing in the daylight.

At night, however, I'd been staring at the sky often, finding the ship's tiny dot of light among the flickering stars. It moved steadily along its orbit, with my commander on board—the man with intense violet eyes and the skin the color of midnight.

The yearning for his arms around me tightened in my chest. I drew in a long breath, reaching for my walking stick after Zenya was gone.

"Hopefully soon," I whispered to myself, getting up.

A shadow moved over the parkette as I limped along the paving stones of the path, as if a large cloud suddenly blocked the bright summer sun.

A man jumped from the bench he'd been sitting on.

"Look!" he yelled, frantically pointing up.

He yanked a cell phone out of his pocket. Holding it in front of him, he started either to film or take pictures.

People in the parkette scurried toward the surrounding buildings.

A woman screamed, cowering.

I tilted my head back. A gasp caught in my throat.

A huge silver disk was blocking the sun. An Ivodian shuttle, shaped like a flying saucer, complete with the spherical shape in the middle, hovered over the skyscrapers that surrounded the parkette.

A wide column of green light descended from the sphere, tinting the air around me lime-green. A figure appeared inside the light.

Wide shoulders. Bald head decorated with rows of piercings. Crisp white uniform that hugged his muscular body in all the right places. Dark purple skin, streaked with lime-green highlights from the column of light. Seven long, flexible tails fanned behind him.

"Brigan..." I exhaled, afraid to believe.

"Run!" someone yelled from the crowd. "Run, lady!"

I smiled.

Why would I run from Brigan? I'd spend weeks dreaming of running *to* him.

My cane slipped from my fingers and clattered to the stone path. I stretched both arms to my alien as he descended in the column of light.

"Lori..." He bent over and grabbed me under my arms.

His tails snaked all around me, binding me to him.

"You," was all I could say, lost in the warm lavender of his gorgeous eyes.

He greedily captured my mouth in a kiss. Hot, messy, and passionate, it was everything I needed.

"I missed you," he groaned against my mouth. "So much, I thought I'd go insane. Hearing your voice today was more than I could take."

"How many laws are you breaking to be here?" I asked, tightening my arms around him. I'd been trying to play by the rules, but I didn't think I could let go of him anymore, even if the entire Universe demanded it.

"None," he grinned. "I ordered the shuttle the moment I heard your voice. One way or another, I was going to come for you today. Lucky for the Coalition, they finally chose to cooperate. No laws have been broken."

He lifted a brow ridge with a glint in his eye.

"I'm abducting you, Lori," he declared. "Legally."

Air left me in a rush. "Legally" meant that no one would take me away from him now.

"Who knew I'd be this happy to get abducted," I laughed as we ascended the column of green light, floating up it, weightless. "Oh," I suddenly remembered. "My cane!"

I reached down to the parkette, from the height of at least a dozen floors already.

"You won't need it, my life." Brigan kissed me again. "On the Conqueror, I'll carry you anywhere you wish to go."

We rose higher and higher, to the highest floors of the downtown skyscrapers. The parkette below was but a patch of green among the asphalt and concrete, now. I held tight to Brigan, even knowing he wouldn't let me fall. His tails wound tightly around me.

They coiled around my legs, my arms, and my middle. One slid under my skirt, slinking around my upper thigh. The tip of the other skimmed the underside of my breast, then slipped inside my neckline. Starved for his touch, I melted into his caress.

Brigan buried his hands in my hair, kissing me just like I'd dreamed he would all this time. Lost in his kiss, I hardly noticed how we boarded the Ivodian shuttle. The green light disappeared, and the floor solidified under our feet.

"Welcome aboard, Captain Soranno," an Ivodian male greeted us.

"Hi," I managed between Brigan's kisses. He wouldn't let go of me.

"Ready for take-off, Commander?" the Ivodian asked.

"Ready," Brigan panted.

Without so much as glancing at the male, he walked me backwards to a wide, padded seat in a shape of a semi-circle along the rounded open space in the middle of the saucer. The control panel, with the pilot taking his seat in front of it, was on the other side of the round room.

Brigan lowered me onto the white cushioned surface, then hit a button on the wall above us. A matte shield rose from the floor, concealing us from the Ivodian at the controls.

"I can't stop touching you," Brigan murmured. His hands didn't stray from my neck and shoulders as he massaged the stress and tension out of my weary muscles.

His tails, however, proved much naughtier than his fingers. Spreading all over my body, they stroked, caressed, and rubbed. The one in my cleavage made its way inside my bra, the tip flicking my nipple. Two others yanked at the front buttons of my blouse, quickly tugging them open.

The tip of one of the tails slid past the waistband of my underwear. I moaned when it brushed by my most sensitive spot between my legs.

"Oh, how I missed this sound." Brigan kissed down my neck, his forked tongue flicking against my flushed skin.

"We don't have much time..." I panted, struggling with the closure of his uniform and wishing I'd had taken a course on how to undress him, too. I needed to feel his skin under my palms.

He quickly slid his fingers along the seam that ran diagonally in front of his shirt. It opened, revealing his smooth, dark skin in the most beautiful shade of night sky.

"I'll use every second we have," he assured me.

I exhaled in pleasure, splaying my hands on the wide expanse of his chest. The pent-up desire for this man raged through me, unleashed by his kisses and caresses. The tip of his tail slid inside me, and I bucked my hips, riding it. Like a deft, nimble finger, it flicked inside me, hitting the spot that drove me wild with need.

"I want you, Brigan. Please," I begged. "I can't... I need..."

Yanking his pants open, he freed his erection. His hot, pulsing length pressed against my thigh. The row of erect "tongues" on top felt slightly more pliable than his hard shaft. They teased my clit as he slid inside me, one tantalizing "lick" after another.

"Oh yes..." I exhaled as he entered me fully, filling me completely.

He leaned back, his eyes roving over me. My blouse was undone, my bra pushed up, with my breasts spilling out, their tips hard and flushed from the touch of his tails.

"I will never get enough of seeing you like this," he rasped, as he gripped my hips, thrusting hard inside me.

I moaned in bliss, my head rolling against the seat. Two of his tails wound around my wrists, yanking my hands over my head. Two others pushed my legs wider apart for him.

I closed my eyes, surrendering to the swells of intense pleasure rolling through me. He took me higher with each of his powerful thrusts until pleasure crested then exploded with shudders of ecstasy. His head tossed back, he roared his release through clenched teeth.

"Come here, Brigan," I called to him, my hands still bound over my head. "Come to me."

He collapsed over me, his tails sliding off my wrists and legs. I wrapped my arms around him, holding him close.

"This is like coming home, Lori. You are my home. My entire life, now."

EPILOGUE

Lori

I woke up to a gentle glide along my inner thigh. Smooth and tantalizing, it felt like the caress of a loving finger, but I knew better. It was a tail. One of Brigan's tails that I simply adored.

Another one eased between my legs while the third one curled around my breast, rubbing against my nipple.

"Mmmm." I rolled to my back, stretching. Sleep retreated slowly as desire took over.

"Morning," the beloved voice of my man whispered, then a kiss landed on my lips.

Brigan.

I arched my back as he trailed his kisses down my chest. A moan escaped me when he sucked one of my nipples in his mouth, his forked tongue teasing and playing with the hardened bud.

His tails roped my knees, pulling them apart. I didn't fight it, opening wide for him.

"Brigan," I breathed out as he dipped his face between my thighs.

"Let me hear more of those moans, my life," he murmured, dragging his tongue between my folds.

I raised my hips to his mouth, riding his tongue. Any remnants of sleep were completely gone now, burned away by the flaming desire. His tails caressed my body, stoking the flames.

He sucked hard, and I came, thrashing against him. His arms around my thighs, he held me in place, sucking and licking every last shudder of pleasure out of me.

Only when I slacked against the mattress did he stop.

"Brigan... This was..." I exhaled in a moan, unable to put into words all the amazing things he'd made me feel.

He licked his lips, pulling himself up along my body.

"I wanted to make sure you start this day right." He grinned. "It's our first full day off."

"Yes, it is." I smiled in return.

It'd been two weeks since the Conqueror left Earth's orbit. With the month I'd spent on the ship before that, I'd been living here for over six weeks now—six crazy busy weeks.

While still in orbit, I helped coordinate the Ivodian-human dating program that had been finally put in place.

The women who had been taken by the Ivodians and wished to give their abductors a second chance got to do so the day after Brigan had plucked me from the parkette near the City Hall in Toronto.

Zenya got to see her Naitas again. And many others were reunited with the aliens they had come to care about, despite how they'd first met.

The Ivodians, whose abducted brides refused to reconcile, had a database created for them. Their profiles had been released to the public, and thousands of women had applied to have a date with each of them. The men then chose just one woman with whom they then got a chance to establish a relationship.

Not everything went smoothly, of course. Some ended up having to go through several rounds of dates before finding *the one*. But at the end of that month, every one of the ninety-seven Ivodians who'd come to Earth to find a bride had been paired with a willing woman, selected through mutual attraction.

During that month, I also had a chance to say goodbye to all my family and friends, promising to visit them as often as I could. The Ivodians' unparalleled achievements in space travel, including the possession of the fastest ships in the Universe, made visiting Earth not only possible, but also something we could do fairly regularly.

"What are we going to do today?" I asked as Brigan propped himself on an elbow at my side.

His tails never left me. Stroking leisurely along my naked body, they kept the desire simmering just beneath my skin.

His eyebrow ridges jerked up, excitement spreading on his face.

"I have a plan," he told me.

Even after all ninety-seven couples had been sorted and the Conqueror left Earth, our lives hadn't slowed down much.

I knew Brigan hadn't planned to retire before he met me. He'd told me he wished to remain with the ship for a few more years to do a few more missions. I didn't want to take that away from him.

Neither was I going to let him travel the Universe without me until he felt ready to retire.

Instead, I'd joined the crew, too. For the past two weeks, I'd been officially training as a pilot of one of the Conqueror's shuttles. I was less than two hundred flying hours away from piloting a flying saucer on my own. The mere thought of it made me giddy.

"So, what's your plan?" I lifted a leg, stretching it, and one of his tails immediately coiled around it several times.

"Well, first, I'm going to make love to you a little more." The tip of another tail circled my right nipple while Brigan played with the left one using his fingers. "Then, we'll have breakfast right here." He tipped his chin at my favorite part of the room—a sitting area in front of the giant window with the spectacular view of the open space beyond.

"I'd love that," I said breathily. The caress of his tails and fingers was setting my blood on fire. Desire throbbed hot between my legs again.

"After that," he continued. "I'll take you to the activity hall and you'll get to choose a few games you want to play."

I'd been to the activity hall briefly during my welcoming tour of the Conqueror. With everything that had been going on, I'd no chance to try it out yet. The hall had an impressive list of virtual imitation games and activities I couldn't wait to test. From simple exercise like jogging on a terrain of any planet imaginable, to recreating famous battles that Ivodians had engaged in throughout history, to virtual dance halls and sightseeing.

"Oh, I want to do all the games and activities," I said enthusiastically.

"You won't be able to do them all in one day," he chuckled, kissing the tip of my nose. "Days wouldn't be enough for that, even if we stayed there around the clock. Besides, I also have dinner planned."

"You do?"

"Mhm. With your favorite dessert."

"Crème Brule?" I gasped. "Really?" I didn't recall ever mentioning my favorite dessert to him. "How did you know?"

Judging by his puzzled expression, he didn't.

"*Crème* what?" he asked, looking dumbfounded. "You said the dessert we had last week was your favorite."

"Oh..."

I remembered the rather nasty combination of caramelized eggplant and grilled tomatoes, drenched in chocolate sauce and sprinkled with mint. The head chef of the Conqueror had been making Ivodian dishes by substituting ingredients with produce from Earth. Sometimes things worked out well. Others... Well, that thing tasted as vile as it sounded.

"You didn't really like it, did you?" Brigan narrowed his eyes at me.

"Um... I'm sorry." I winced.

"Why did you say you did, then?"

I scratched my ear, stalling my answer.

"I didn't really say I liked it. I said it was nice, just trying to be polite."

"Lori," he groaned, grabbing my shoulders. "You have to be absolutely honest with me about these things. I ordered a huge part of our gardens planted with eggplants and tomatoes. Just because you said you liked that dish."

"Wow... Really?" I stared at him in shock.

"Sweetheart. You don't understand," he said softly, leaning closer. "If you tell me you like something, I'll go through the fiery pits of Ahell to make sure it's available to you at a moment's notice. You are my wife, Lori. Making you happy is my mission in life."

I'd noticed Brigan going out of his way to please me. Pretending to like the nasty dessert had been a mistake.

"I'm sorry." I cupped his face. "I promise I'll be more careful next time." I placed a peck on his cheek. "But don't worry, the tomatoes and eggplants you planted aren't going to waste. I know a few great recipes with them that you may like, provided I put enough pepper in the pot, of course," I added with an apologetic smile.

He kissed me, then reached for his comm device on the night table.

"What are you doing?" I asked.

"I'll need to tell the head chef to change the dessert for dinner tonight. What did you say your favorite was? *Crème* something?" He shook his head. "I can't believe I'm only learning this now."

Oh boy. I imagined the head chef scrambling in the galley, trying to recreate an Earth dessert, the ingredients for which he might not even have readily available.

I moved his hand away from the comm.

"Don't worry about it." I twined my arms around Brigan's neck, climbing into his lap. "The only thing I absolutely demand about tonight's dinner is you being there with me."

"I'm not going anywhere." The concern on his face softened as I kissed his jaw. "I'm not leaving your side now, Lori."

"Good." I nibbled down the corded muscles of his neck with a series of kisses. Straddling his thighs, I felt his erection growing against my core. "I love your plan for today, Commander. What was the first point, again?"

"Making love," he groaned, shifting me closer.

I rubbed my core along his hard length. The row of his erect tongue-petals dragged between my heated folds. I sucked in a breath. Desire coursed through me in hot ripples of pleasure.

"I'll never say no to your lovemaking," I murmured as he slid inside me.

"WHERE EXACTLY ARE YOU taking me?" I asked, hurrying alongside Brigan.

The ship was enormous. After six weeks here, I still only had a vague idea of its actual size and all the amenities it had to offer.

My leg had completely healed by now. I needed neither a cane to walk nor Brigan to carry me anywhere anymore. Though he had still carried me to the shower that morning, just because he liked doing that, and after all the lovemaking I was too happy to oblige.

"Where are we going for dinner?"

"You'll see," he said, a mysterious smile playing on his lips. He touched a panel on the wall and it slid back, opening into a dark room beyond. The space was illuminated only by the distant stars twinkling outside of the giant glass dome of a ceiling.

Stepping over the threshold, I lifted the hem of my purple-silk gown, lest I trip over it in my silver heels—just a few of the many beautiful things Brigan had insisted on buying for me before we left Earth.

"Happy Birthday, Lori," he whispered in my ear.

Lights suddenly burst to life, illuminating the huge room with dozens of round tables in the middle.

"Happy Birthday!" The air erupted with cheers as humans and Ivodians jumped up from behind the tables.

"What?" I gasped in shock, clutching Brigan's hand in mine.

Today wasn't my birthday, but it sure felt nice to have a party.

"Surprise!" He grinned, pleased as could be. "You never got a proper celebration, my life. And you deserve the best there is. Happy belated birthday."

"This is...for me?" I slowly turned around, taking in the room, brightly decorated with balloons, flowers I'd never seen before, and ribbons.

A huge *"Happy Birthday, Lori"* banner, with the words spelled in English, hung under the glass ceiling. A long table to the side held a giant teddy bear surrounded by an enormous pile of wrapped presents.

"For you, my love, my sweetheart, my life." Taking me in his arms, Brigan punctuated every sweet word of endearment with a kiss.

"But how did you manage to do all of this?" I laughed, shaking my head—happy but still in shock. "When?"

"I've had help," he murmured, holding me close.

Zenya waved at me from behind the nearest table, with Naitas holding her arm. There were many happy human-Ivodian couples in the room. Even the first engineer wasn't alone. Advika, his new bride, smiled next to him, her dark skin glowing on her cheeks, a long black braid draped over her shoulder. She gazed at her husband adoringly as he poured her a glass of wine.

"Do you like it?" Brigan asked, sweeping the room in one arm gesture.

"I love it!" I gushed. "I just can't believe it. How did you pull it off? I mean, even with help..."

"I did some extensive research on human celebrations and traditions, specifically in your home region of North America."

"You did good." I couldn't stop smiling. "Simply amazing."

Things got mixed up a little during his research, it appeared. The teddy bear was holding a stuffed red heart in his paws with the words *Be Mine!* embroidered on it. Brigan must've mixed up birthday and Valentine's Day a little. Not that I minded. A giant teddy bear was something I never knew I wanted badly.

"I really, really love it, Brigan." My eyes got misty from all the happy emotions bursting in my chest like fireworks.

"Zenya told me the words on the heart in the stuffed animal's paws say 'Be mine.' It felt like a fitting message." He lifted me in his arms, carrying me to the central table. "You're mine."

"As you are mine, Brigan." I wrapped my arms around his strong neck.

"Oh, I've been yours all along, my life. You've abducted me. You've claimed me. From that moment, I never stood a chance."

Bonus Epilogue

Thank you for reading My Birthday Getaway.

I had a hard time saying goodbye to Lori and Brigan after I've finished writing My Birthday Getaway.

I wondered how Lori was adjusting to her new life. I wanted to see what Brigan's property on Us'ae, one of Rimall's three moons, looked like. But most of all, I wanted Brigan to tell us how he lost his tail.

If you're also curious about all those things, I have a short story on my Patreon with all the answers. It's available to read on all tiers:

More in My Holiday Tails Series

New Year, New Planet

Tessa

"Everyone needs an adventure in their lives, Tessa!" Bree yelled from the common area of our apartment.

"I have enough adventures," I yelled back from behind the partially closed doors of my bedroom. "Dammit, my entire life is an adventure."

I've been traveling for a living most of my adult life. We were in the City of Voran, on Neron, a planet only a handful of people from Earth had had a chance to visit. Wasn't that an adventure already?

After closing the tiny hooks on the side of my black-and-white, polka-dot skirt I zipped up the zipper.

"I'm on an alien planet, Bree. How much more of an adventure can it be?"

Before taking the job that had brought me to Neron, I'd worked on several luxury yachts back home on Earth. Their owner rented the yachts to whoever could pay the hefty price. As a steward, I'd travelled with the crew all over the Caribbean and the Mediterranean.

"Your life is not an adventure, Tessa," Bree argued. "Because you don't actually *live* it. You work. And when you have time off, you read in your cabin. You have every chance for an adventure, but you never take it. It makes no difference that you're on a spaceship or on another planet. You don't go out. You see nothing. You may as well be back on Earth in some shitty small town, working in a hole-in-the-wall diner. You don't *live* the adventure, you skirt right by it."

Her words scraped unpleasantly inside me. It hurt. Probably because Bree was right. I preferred to stay safe.

My very first job actually was in a diner. My biological parents weren't in the picture since my birth. My foster family had made sure I'd been fed and clothed while growing up. But once I turned eighteen, they gave me a suitcase and wished me a happy life.

I wasn't angry with them. They'd helped me get my driver's licence, my first job, and my first apartment. They still emailed me a Christmas card every year. But once I'd left their house, I'd always known I had no one but myself to count on in this life.

As a waitress in a diner, I'd worked hard, taking as many shifts as was physically possible. One night, a customer had witnessed me resolving a nasty situation at three in the morning—a drunk was harassing another waitress. The witness had been impressed with the way I handled it. He had turned out to be the owner of several luxury yachts that he rented to wealthy clients, and he'd offered me a job on the service crew.

Since then, my life had become a string of trips, ports, and endless travels.

Brie was right, however. I preferred to play it safe. I'd been to many countries, but had hardly experienced their culture. I rarely met new people, and preferred to stay in my cabin, reading.

"Come on, Tessa," Bree exclaimed. "We're on a freaking alien planet, girl! You need to live a little."

I smoothed my hands over my dark hair then closed the tiny silver buckles of my black mary-jane shoes and grabbed my purse.

"I'm trying." I stepped out of my bedroom into our living room that burst with vines and flowers in the typical Voranian fashion. "I've agreed to come with you on this double-date, haven't I?"

My lifestyle wasn't conducive to building and maintaining relationships, but sometimes loneliness got the best of me. Going out and meeting new people made me feel more excited than apprehensive this time. New Year's Eve was my favorite holiday, and I was looking forward to the party.

Bree gave me a measuring look, taking in my outfit of a cup-sleeved blouse, flared polka-dot skirt, and black heels.

"What?" I ran my hands down my skirt, feeling self-conscious under her scrutiny.

Bree was dressed in a gorgeous mid-thigh-length dress with open back that complemented her golden-red hair in a most stunning way.

Unlike me, Bree made sure never to miss an adventure. She also never failed to tell Lucy and me about her escapades. Lucy, another woman from Earth, came to Neron with our ship and was sharing the apartment with Bree and me.

Lucy was sitting on a white couch in front of the large, white-screen TV. A Voranian movie was playing, but she had it on mute, listening to our conversation instead.

Bree yanked my sleeves down to expose my shoulders.

"Not too bad, but something is missing..." she muttered, staring at me like I was a picture in a museum and she was trying to appraise me. "I see you're going for a kind of a sexy librarian look. Sweet and smart. That's good. Guys like it."

Was *that* what I was going for? I just put on the only skirt I owned that wasn't a part of my uniform.

"Red lipstick is great. But this purse needs to go." Bree tugged at the hard-shell bag I had in the crook of my elbow. "Get rid of it."

I clutched the handles tighter. "My purse? No way. My entire life is in it."

Bree wouldn't let go, though.

"You don't need to bring your entire life on a date." Leave it here. It makes you look like a librarian."

"But you just said guys liked that look!" I protested.

She blew out a breath, clearly exasperated with my being so clueless. "Men want a 'librarian on vacation.' A demure, quiet girl ready to let loose. This purse says a 'librarian at work'—the one who's more likely to hiss at them to be quiet than let them ravage her."

Did I want to get "ravaged" by someone?

Living a proper life had kept me safe and mostly out of trouble. Sometimes it got excruciatingly lonely, though.

I had no family. The only friends I had were my co-workers. Like most people in this world, I often longed for a connection. In my case, however, that could only be a very short-lived connection before I was off to another port, country, or planet. Even that happened rarely. It'd been over a year since a man had last held me in his arms.

"Fine..." I set the purse on a side table by the couch. "But I need these two things from it." I took out my glasses and my wallet.

"You don't need the wallet. I have the invites." Bree flashed two glossy, hologram-enhanced cards to me. "These will pay for food and drinks."

"But my glasses..." I held on to my red, cat-eye frame.

My farsightedness wasn't bad. I needed glasses to drive, to be able to read the street signs and such, but I went around without them otherwise. I liked having them with me, though. It made me feel more confident and secure.

Bree squinted at the glasses in my hands, tapping her chin with her finger.

"Let me see." She took them from me then perched them on my nose.

I immediately slid my finger up the bridge of my nose, adjusting the position of the glasses.

"You know? I don't hate it," she announced, giving me a critical once-over again. "They look rather trendy, go well with that sexy librarian thing, and add a splash of much needed color."

I caught my reflection in the floor-to-ceiling window. The sun had long set. The dark sky outside turned the glass of the window into a navy-blue mirror.

At almost five feet ten inches, I was taller than most women I knew. There was nothing dainty or delicate about my body, either. I had strong shoulders that looked even more prominent now that Bree had exposed them. My hips pushed the soft folds of the skirt out. I had a well-defined waist but nowhere thin enough for a man to circle it with his hands—no hour-glass figure here.

"It's cute, Tessa." Lucy said softly, tucking a strand of her blond hair behind her ear. "You look beautiful."

"Thank you."

Unlike Bree and me, Lucy wasn't a flight attendant. She worked for the human branch of the Earth-Voran Liaison Committee, the organization that was in charge of any joint projects between humans and Voranians. That included the marriage program that started several years ago and the transportation operations that had begun with it. As part of a crew operating a spaceship from Earth, Bree and I fell under their control, too.

Lucy's assignment on this trip was to travel to the planet Aldrai. The Aldraians had recently expressed an interest in a marriage program with humans, and Lucy's task was to evaluate their planet as a suitable environment for our men and women.

Unlike Voraninas, who had a severe shortage of females due to their birth rate being heavily skewed in favor of males, Aldraians had a healthy balance between males and females born.

Their interest in humans as spouses had other reasons. Aldraian pregnancies were few but resulted in a large number of babies born to one woman. By mixing the genes, they hoped to achieve more frequent pregnancies but with fewer babies. It would significantly improve Aldraian female health, without a drop in population growth, and give a chance to more couples to start a family.

Unlike the Voranians, whose marriage agreement with us involved only women, Aldraians were looking at opening their program to both women and men.

"You need more color..." Bree muttered under her breath.

She plucked a red flower from the nearest vine and stuck it behind my ear.

"Here." She leaned back, admiring the results of her work. "That's better. Guys around here adore flowers."

Winter lasted almost six months in Voran. But Voranians loved summer, and decorated their living spaces with an abundance of living plants.

The apartment where the three of us stayed was located in the building of the Liaison Committee. The inside looked like a real garden, with garlands of flowers dripping from the walls and ceilings. Pots with tall lattices of vines served as partitions throughout the living areas. And a sophisticated Artificial Intelligence system oversaw the maintenance of this indoor paradise.

People of Voran had adapted the methods of Aldraians of growing and tending to plants. The Voranians adored greenery. Aldraians must love it even more. From the little I knew about Aldrai, it was a garden planet. People literally lived in their gardens there. They didn't even bother with building houses.

The two men that Bree had arranged for a double-date with us tonight had come from Aldrai.

I touched the flower above my ear.

"He'll love it," she assured me.

She'd only met one of the men. Once.

The two Aldraians had come to Neron for business and were staying in a hotel nearby. Bree ran into one of them in a café in a glass covered walkway that connected the hotel with our building. They'd chatted. As it'd turned out both men had received the invitations to the New Year Celebration event organized by the Liaison Committee, too. In a moment of weakness, I'd promised I'd come to keep the second guy company.

I'd never met an Aldraian before. The whole aspect of a blind date was nerve-racking on its own. Add to that the fact that the man was an alien from a planet where no human had even been to yet... Well, my hands turned sweaty every time I thought about it and my heart thundered so loudly, I feared a heart attack.

Unlike me, Bree looked rather bouncy. Her green eyes shone with excitement.

"Are you sure you don't want to come with us, Lucy?" she asked.

"No. Thank you." Lucy shook her head, adjusting the elastic waistband of her sweatpants. "My flight is tomorrow morning. I need to get some rest."

Bree laughed. "Mine too!"

Our spaceship was leaving for Aldrai at nine in the morning. Because we only had one passenger on this flight—Lucy—only one flight attendant was required to accompany it. Bree was scheduled to work tomorrow. But it hadn't stopped her from accepting the invitation to the event tonight.

"Sleep is overrated." Bree headed for the door. "Are you ready to have some fun, Tessa?"

"Sure." With a wave at Lucy and a longing glance at her comfy position on the couch, I followed Bree out of the apartment.

"So, you've never seen an Aldraian before?" Bree asked as we walked down a long hallway to the glass-tube elevator.

"No." Aldraians never came to Earth. And there weren't many of them here, on Neron. "I mean I've seen pictures of them, once or twice."

The images were blurry in my memory. I recalled the males of that species had horns, and women had three pairs of breasts—due to the births of multiples, I assumed.

"Well." Bree chewed on her bottom lip. "Their men are not what people would call 'pretty boys.' You know?"

"What do you mean?"

"Well, Ravils and Ivodians are hot, right?"

"Sure."

I'd only seen people of both of these species on TV, but like most of the Universe, I too found them attractive. Ravils's had thick, golden manes of hair, and their muscular bodies were covered in short velvety fur. Ivodian were generally tall, dark, and handsome, with nine long, graceful tails.

Bree made a face, tilting her head. "Well, you wouldn't call Voranians beautiful, either, come to think of it."

Voranians were very much scary-looking, with their horns, hooves, and charcoal fur. Yet I found many of them agreeable. Alcus Hecear, the Voranian representative of the Liaison Committee whom we'd interacted with the most, was really charming. I liked him a lot.

We stopped in front of the elevator and I pressed the button. "There's nothing wrong with Voranians. They're nice people."

"So, you're okay with horns?" Bree asked.

"Sure. Why not?"

She squinted at me as we stepped in the elevator. "I mean like a *lot* of horns?"

"What are you talking about?"

She bit her lip. "Aldrarians look...different. I just don't want you to be disappointed."

I shrugged. "I honestly don't care about their looks."

Going on a blind date with an alien, one had to expect something different, right?

"Listen," I said. "It's not like I'm going to marry the guy. I'm just there to keep him company while you're...doing whatever it is you're going to do with the other one. And anyway, looks don't matter as long as they're decent people."

The elevator stopped and its doors opened.

"Right." A mischievous spark flashed in Bree's eyes. "Though, I rather hope Prug isn't going to be *decent* with me tonight."

AVAILABLE NOW

More by Marina Simcoe

The World of the River of Mists

Call of Water
Madness of the Moon
Power of Rage

Paranormal Romance

<u>Demons (Complete Series)</u>
Demon Mine
The Forgotten
Grand Master
The Last Unforgiven - Cursed
The Last Unforgiven - Freed

<u>Stand Alone Novels Set in Demons World</u>
The Real Thing
To Love A Monster

<u>Midnight Coven Author Group</u>
Wicked Warlock (Cursed Coven)

About the Author

Marina Simcoe likes to write love stories with characters, who may or may not be entirely human, because she firmly believes that our contemporary world could always use a little bit of the extraordinary.

She has lots of fun exploring how her out-of-this-world characters with their own beliefs, values, and aspirations fit into our every-day life.

She lives in Canada with her very own grumpy brute, their three little kids, and a cat, who is definitely out of this world.

To see illustration to some of the author's books and more, please join her Patreon:

Please Stay in Touch

Newsletter signup is on MarinaSimcoe.com:

Facebook Readers' Group:
Marina's Reading Cave
www.instagram.com/marinasimcoeauthor
www.marinasimcoe.com
www.facebook.com/MarinaSimcoeAuthor/
www.amazon.com/author/marinasimcoe
www.bookbub.com/profile/marina-simcoe
www.goodreads.com/MarinaSimcoe